Rutherford's WOMAN
A Family Legacy

2

A NOVEL BY

L.J. BOWEN

Copyright © 2018

Published by Major Key Publishing

www.majorkeypublishing.com

ALL RIGHTS RESERVED.

Any unauthorized reprint or use of the material is prohibited. No part of this book may be reproduced or transmitted in any form or by any means, electronic, or mechanical, including photocopying, recording, or by any information storage without express permission by the publisher.

This is an original work of fiction. Names, characters, places and incidents are either products of the author's imagination or are used fictitiously and any resemblance to actual persons, living or dead is entirely coincidental.

Contains explicit language & adult themes suitable for ages 16+

❋ Created with Vellum

JOIN MAJOR KEY!

To submit a manuscript for our review, email us at
submissions@majorkeypublishing.com

10 YEARS LATER...

Jemma finished making her chart notes at the nurse's station in the emergency room department and put them in the doctor's intake bin to be signed.

"And I am officially done," she said with a smile as one of her coworkers, Gary, walked up to the desk and leaned against it.

"You don't have to rub it in. Ready to go?" he asked, and she nodded.

"Yes, let me run these x-rays upstairs, and I'll meet you outside," she replied, grabbing the films and heading toward the elevators.

As she waited for the elevator in the ER area, she was glad to be getting away from the hospital for a few days. She hadn't had a real vacation since she started working at the hospital six years ago. She loved being a nurse at Mercy Heart in Chicago. It was a busy U-shaped tan and white building that catered from emergency services to podiatry. It was one of the busiest hospitals in the city, and like many similar facilities, it focused on patient care and health management. Jemma had graduated at the top of her class and decided to get a double certification in obstetrics. She mostly worked in the ER, but if needed, she would work in the labor and delivery ward. It took a lot of training and discipline to not get emotional when she saw people in pain or hurt, but she put forth proficient care to take care of the patients. She was a damn good nurse, and the administrators at Mercy Heart knew it. The elevator arrived, and she saw Dr. Langham on it, releasing a smile.

"Nurse Alden."

"Dr. Langham, how are you?"

He was a young resident who had worked at the hospital for about a year, and she thought he was cute. Even though she had that opinion, she never dated co-workers. She didn't want to have an uncomfortable work environment if the relationship didn't work out. Evan Langham was a medium height man with a sand-colored complexion, average features, and was in the beginning stages of growing out dreadlocks. He was very respectful and valued her expertise as a colleague.

"I'm fine. How are you? I thought you were leaving this nut house for a few days." She chuckled at that, and he smiled.

"I see word still travels fast around here. I am, but I wanted to drop off these x-rays first."

"You know this place can function without you being a super nurse," Dr. Langham mentioned matter-of-factly with a smile, and she laughed again.

"I know. I just like to make sure all my work is done before I leave."

"I understand. You're flying to Atlanta, right?"

"Yes. My best friend is getting married, and I'm the maid of honor."

"That should be fun."

"Yeah. I'm excited about it." The elevator doors opened, and she stepped off. "You have a good day, Dr. Langham."

"You too, Jemma. Enjoy your trip."

"Thank you." She smiled again and waved to him. Evan made a mental note to ask Jemma out on a date when he saw her again.

She dropped the films off on the cardiology floor and stopped in the employee lounge to grab her purse and luggage. She saw Gary in his white Ford and climbed into the passenger seat after placing her suitcase in the trunk.

"Thanks again for taking me to the airport." Gary waved her words away and got on Lake Shore Drive to head toward Midway Airport.

"It's fine. Now, honey, when you get to *Hotlanta*, you have to promise me you're going to have fun and get dicked down really good," Gary told her, and she looked at him like he was insane.

He had a pinch of a Latin accent and had a husky build. In addition to being co-workers, they had attended their last year of nursing school together and had become good friends.

"Well, seeing as though I'm the maid of honor, that's probably the last thing on my to-do list," she responded, enjoying the breeze that was coming through the open windows.

Jemma unquestionably loved Chicago in the summertime. There was always something to do and places to visit. The city was especially abuzz because of how good the Bulls did in the playoffs, and everyone was still talking about it.

"I'm sure you can squeeze in a quickie with a wedding guest." She laughed at that and shook her head.

"What do you and Tony have planned for tonight?" Tony was Gary's partner and a well-known DJ in the city.

"Well, he's playing at MB's tonight, and I'm chilling since I have to be at work at six in the morning. I'm serious about that quickie. It is not natural or healthy to go without sex. You have to use the lady parts you were given. How long has it been?"

"Heck, I don't know, Gary. I'm not counting that time with Arnold, so who knows?" she replied, causing him to giggle.

"Oh, I forgot about the crybaby."

"Please don't remind me."

She briefly remembered Arnold, whom she dated three years ago. When they finally decided to have sex, it was over before it got started. He literally cried afterward, and she spent the rest of the night comforting him with constant eye rolls and sighs. Jemma had broken up with him the next day and hadn't given him another thought.

"Honestly, I'm just going to go there, girl talk with my BFF, and have fun at her wedding."

Jemma still couldn't believe that Sonya was marrying Brandon

Drake of all people given the love/hate relationship they had in college. She sighed, not wanting to think about that time. She didn't want to think about it… about him… She didn't want to reflect on Will Rutherford and how she had never gotten over him and probably never would, but she knew she had to for her mental well-being. She was doing well, though. This was the first time she thought about Will in years and figured it might be appropriate since half of the people getting married had been his friend in school. Jemma shook her head to clear away those thoughts since she would never see him again. The last time Jemma had spoken to Sonya, she specifically asked if Will was going to be at the wedding, and Sonya told her she didn't think so because he hadn't RSVP'd. As they got closer to the airport, the traffic slowed down. Gary found her terminal and turned on the hazard lights to let Jemma out. She kissed him on his cheek, grabbed her luggage, and walked into the busy airport.

WILL SAT down on a comfortable black leather cushioned chair in the first-class lounge as he dialed the number to his office. It was a quiet, spacious room with wide, tall windows, a well-stocked bar with chrome bar seats and matching furniture that set on a gray patterned carpet. A few people were present, and he had a thirty-minute layover in Chicago to Atlanta, so he decided to call his secretary Mrs. Lopez.

"William Rutherford's office. Fiona speaking. How can I help you?"

"Hi, Fiona."

She huffed out a breath, and he grinned, catching the eye of the first-class lounge attendant.

"Mr. Rutherford, you know the purpose of going away is to enjoy oneself," she explained in a motherly tone, and he rolled his eyes.

"I am enjoying myself. I have a layover, and I'm calling to check on things."

"Everything is going great. Your office with the firm in Chicago will be set up and ready for you when you get back. All court documents have been sent, and all of your clients have been reassigned to new lawyers. You're the best man at your friend's wedding... relax and cut loose."

Will had accepted the junior associate position at the Kane, Green, and Fry law firm in Chicago. Talks and relocation negotiations had been going on for months, and he was excited about the move. He was eager to sharpen his claws at a new firm. Just under thirty, Will knew he'd have to prove his worth. Will didn't want to leave anything to chance, so he had taken the bar exam for Illinois and was now able to practice law in two states. He was as tall as he'd been in his college days but had gotten sinewy from his time spent at the gym, and he was now sporting a nicely trimmed goatee.

He had paid a hefty price to have a house located for him in Illinois, and from the numerous calls and emails from his realtor, he was happy with the house she had found in Country Club Hills after seeing the pictures. He had flown in to see it a few weeks before and had gone through the process of having it inspected and making sure it had no liens on it. Will still couldn't believe Brandon and Sonya were getting hitched, especially since they didn't get along in college. He absolutely refused to think about certain parts of his college years. He didn't want to think about Jemma and wasn't going to give that hazel-eyed heartbreaker another thought.

He was hoping that she wouldn't make an appearance at the wedding due to an illness or something. Brandon had been honest with Will and told him that an invitation had been sent to Jemma and Will was not pleased with the news. *Hell, who was he to tell them who not to invite to their wedding?* She might show up, but that didn't mean he had to deal with her.

"Trust me, Mr. Rutherford, everything is fine here," she reassured him as she was taping up a box.

"I do trust you, Fiona."

She had been his secretary for years, and he refused to not have her accompany him to Chicago. Fiona was a short, Mexican, and buxom woman who was bilingual and always kept her long brown hair in a low ponytail. She was a widow, and her only daughter lived in Hawaii with her husband, so there was nothing holding her in

Washington. She was looking forward to moving to a new city as well. She had years under her belt as a legal secretary; not to mention, she was efficient and knowledgeable.

"OK, I won't bother you again while I'm away," Will told her, and she chuckled while shaking her head.

"Yeah, right. I'm expecting a least one more call from you."

They exchanged goodbyes before disconnecting the call, and Will sat back in the chair to enjoy his newspaper and coffee. The hot beverage had become his lifeline while going through law school and studying for the bar.

"Excuse me, Mr. Rutherford." The blonde lounge attendant who had given him a smoldering look earlier walked over to him with a smile on her face.

"Yes?"

"They're getting ready to board first class passengers for your flight to Atlanta," she informed him, and he stood up.

"OK, great. Thank you."

"You're more than welcome," She responded with a teasing glint in her eyes.

JEMMA SHUFFLED her items around in her tote bag, looking for the extra batteries for her cd player.

"Dang it. I forgot them," she whispered.

She was sitting down on one of the beige plastic chairs outside the gate to her airplane. Her luggage had been checked, and she was all set for her flight. She had a copy of the latest *Ebony* magazine in her bag, so she'd have something to read since she couldn't listen to her electronic device. She saw a little girl staring at the blue and pink teddy bears on her scrubs, and she smiled. As usual, the airport was busy with people flying in and out of the city. She saw people walking at a leisurely pace or running to get to their next connection. Posted security guards were around the facility, and that eased the environment for the travelers. An announcement came over the PA that the flight to her destination was starting to board, and she gathered her things to stand up. A hard, male body colliding into her caused Jemma to stumble to the left as a large hand reached out to steady her.

"Oh!"

"Excuse me. You jumped up so fast, I didn't see you. Are you okay?" She readjusted her bag in her shoulder and looked up to reassure the man she was fine when she gasped loudly.

"Will!"

"Jemma?"

She noticed that he had snatched his hand away like she had the plague, and she felt like she was about to pass out. Everything literally moved around them at a slow pace as spots danced before her eyes while they continued to eyeball each other. Her heart was beating like a bongo drum, and it felt like it was about to pound right out of her chest. *What the hell?*

Will's eyes roamed over Jemma, not believing she was standing in front of him. Clearly, his eyes were playing tricks on him. He took in her nursing attire, and a small shard of him so tiny he didn't even acknowledge it, was proud that she had become what she went to school for. The air seemed to get hot around them, the intensity of their proximity made them become very aware of each other. She had never had a man look at her like Will was doing now, and it was very unnerving.

"What are you doing here?" Her voice came out squeaky, and she cleared her throat.

"Getting on an airplane; we *are* at the airport." She flinched at his tone and harsh words and took a deep breath. His comment accompanied the severity of his gaze, and she didn't know how to respond to it.

"I didn't mean… Forget it." She closed her mouth and bit her bottom lip since she honestly didn't know what to say to him.

His eyes narrowed when he saw her movement, and he felt a tightness grip on his heart.

"Excuse me." Will pushed past her and headed toward the gate. Jemma did not believe that they were on the same flight.

"Crap!"

She waited for a few seconds before following. Her stomach quivered with nerves. Will looked back and saw Jemma walking a few feet behind him on the jet bridge with people between them. Their eyes met, and she saw him frown again. Once everyone was settled, the plane took off after the in-flight directions and safety procedures were discussed. Jemma closed her eyes and tried to stabilize her breathing. She was sitting in coach with a window view. It was semi-full, and luckily, the seat was empty between her and the tall woman sitting in the next seat.

Jemma recalled the last five minutes; Will's face swam in her head. He still looked good… *so freaking good!* It didn't take a genius to figure out that he was going to the wedding. Jemma was going to slap Sonya's face when she saw her for not mentioning that Will was going to be at the wedding. She couldn't get the look of hatred he had given her out her head.

In retrospect, if anything, she should be the one who had contempt for Will. She sighed and threw her head back. *This is going to be the longest five days ever…*

Will watched the clouds go by the window, still trying to wrap his head around the fact that Jemma was on the same flight. He was going to punch Brandon's lights out when he saw him for not saying anything about Jemma. It wasn't like they hadn't talked several times before the wedding date had arrived. *Fuck, she looks good*, he thought. No matter how much he hated the sight of her, he knew they had to be congenial for the bride and groom. He realized that he would only deal with Jemma if he had to. Given that it was Wednesday, and the wedding wasn't until Saturday, he prayed he wouldn't need a steady flow of alcoholic beverages to get through the next few days.

CHAPTER 1

The plane landed in Georgia with ease. They got their luggage and headed outside to the cab area without speaking another word to each other. There were shadowy clouds in the sky, looking like rain would fall within minutes. They took separate cabs to the Crown Peaks Plaza Hotel on the outskirts of the downtown area within minutes of shopping outlets and tourist attractions. The hotel was twenty-five stories with four grand ballrooms, a restaurant, a lounge with a full-scale bar, trolley services, an Olympic sized swimming pool, a business center, and a state-of-the-art gym. After Jemma checked in, she took the elevator up to the fifteenth floor where her suite was located. Opening the door, Jemma was impressed by the size of it. Concrete gray plush carpet lined the room, with a queen size bed that had a lavender and ivory colored comforter and six fluffy pillows.

A large TV was mounted on the wall above the oak dresser, there was a small sofa and matching chair with a jacuzzi in the decent size bathroom that held all the hotel amenities. Sonya's dad, who was now a senator, had paid for the rooms for the bridal party. Sonya was his only child, and he was sparing no expense for the wedding. His only request was that she keep the revelry small, which was why Jemma,

Sonya's cousin, and sorority sister made up the bridal party. She unpacked her clothes and sat down on the bed to call Sonya, who had given Jemma her room and phone number before she left Chicago.

"Hello?"

"Hey, bride."

"Jemma! You made it!" Sonya exclaimed, and Jemma grinned.

"Yep, I just unpacked my things."

"Come down to my room. I'm in 1507."

Jemma hung up, grabbed her room key, and left the room just as it started pouring outside. She saw the correct room at the end of the hall and didn't get an opportunity to knock before the door was yanked open. The two women hugged each other with excitement, both glad to see each other since it had almost been a year since their last visit.

"Girl, look at you!" Sonya said.

"Look at you... about to get married and everything." Jemma hit her shoulder softly with a genuine smile.

"I know. I'll be glad when it's over. These last few weeks have been stressful."

They went to sit on the couch while the weather channel was showing on TV in the background. Sonya still looked the same, but she donned a cute pixie cut, and her figure looked shapely, even in a red t-shirt and long blue jean skirt.

"Where are your parents?" Jemma asked as she settled back on the couch.

"Our moms are meeting with the wedding planner, and the fathers are out with some of dad's golf buddies."

"Why aren't you meeting with the wedding planner?" Jemma asked, slipping her shoes off.

"Mom wanted me to relax tonight, and I agreed with her. You know how she can get," Sonya replied, and Jemma giggled, nodding her head. Mrs. Augustine wasn't a woman to argue with when she got going. Jemma reached over and slapped Sonya on her arm.

"Ow! What was that for?"

"You didn't tell me Will was coming to the wedding."

"Oh... let me tell you what happened. He confirmed his RSVP at the last minute, and I didn't get a chance to tell you with everything that was going on. He's the best man," Sonya commented with wide eyes, and Jemma smirked at her.

"Are you serious?"

"What? Let's order room service, and we'll talk about it."

Jemma shot daggers with her eyes as Sonya skipped across the room to the phone and rolled her eyes when Sonya gave her the OK sign.

∽

"I SHOULD PUNCH your fucking lights out, but I don't want Sonya mad at me for you having a black eye," Will told Brandon, who had just walked into Will's suite.

"Whoa! What type of greeting is that from my best man?"

"Why didn't you tell me Jemma was going to be here?" Will had taken off his suit jacket and undid his tie.

"Oh, that... let me tell you what happened. I knew, but I didn't want to tell you in case you didn't show up." Will charged toward Brandon, who threw his hands up after reciting the line he and Sonya had rehearsed.

"Hey! Don't hit my face, man! We have pictures to take."

Brandon had on khaki pants and a royal blue button-down shirt. Like Will, he also had gotten bulkier since leaving college, and he seemed a lot happier.

"You suck at warning people, dude. You could've said, 'hey, by the way, the girl who broke your heart ten years ago is in my wedding party,'" Will stated, snatching off the necktie. Brandon saw how this was affecting Will, and he felt bad. Brandon should've told Will, but he didn't want his friend to not show up and celebrate his wedding because his ex would be in attendance. He patted Will on the back and offered an apology.

"I'm sorry, Will. I didn't know it was still an issue with you," Brandon said while looking at Will, who shrugged.

"It's not. Trust me," he replied in a dismissive tone.

"Hey, Robert should be here by now. Let's go have dinner. The three of us can talk and catch up." The news that his brother was nearby perked Will up, and it brought him out of his brooding mood.

∼

"Wow. That must have been one hell of a plane ride," Sonya said, drinking her lemon water. She had ordered a chicken salad, and Jemma had gotten a turkey sandwich with a small order of fries. Jemma nodded as she finished off the last bite of the food.

"That is your last fatty meal until the wedding. Final fittings are tomorrow, and we're not letting out your dress, missy."

"Don't worry. I'm going to that gym downstairs to work off this food and anxiety tonight."

"So, how does he look?" Sonya asked with a sly grin.

It had been some years since she had seen Will but knew he and Brandon had met up together a few times over the years. Jemma sighed before answering, pushing the plate away. She was hoping that question wouldn't be asked so she'd have to answer it.

"Fine. Sexy as hell… harder. He has a goatee that adds to his handsomeness. I swear, I wish things had turned out differently for us."

Jemma answered the question. The last part was a whimper, and Sonya felt sympathy for her friend, especially since she knew how crazy in love they were in college. Sonya intentionally didn't tell Jemma that Will was coming so she wouldn't use that as an excuse to not show up. Call her selfish, but she wanted her best friend here to witness her marrying the man of her dreams.

"Maybe since the two of you are here, it will give you a chance to hash out some grievances," Sonya suggested as Jemma shook her head while taking a sip of her lemonade.

"It is what it is, but that is enough about me. What's on the agenda for you? I'm the maid of honor. What do you need me to do?" Jemma wouldn't monopolize the time talking about her past with Will. There was a wedding coming up, and that took precedence over everything else.

"My cousin Carla and sorority sister Sandi will be here later tonight, and you're going to love them. Tomorrow we'll get up, have breakfast, have our final fittings, go get our accessories, and pick up the ring. Friday will be the rehearsal dinner. I'm having a spa party for us where we'll be pampered and massaged Friday night. Makeup and hair will start at ten on Saturday morning. The wedding is starting at three sharp! I don't care who is here or not," Sonya emphasized, and Jemma smiled.

"Ooh! You're scrappy... I like that." Sonya burst out laughing and shoved Jemma.

"Shut up."

"Sounds good. Since we'll be out tomorrow, I can pick up your wedding gift."

"Oh! What is it? Tell me."

"Umm... no. Speaking of gifts, I haven't seen any. Where are they? I thought some of them would have arrived by now."

"My parents are holding them hostage in their room like I can't be trusted with the presents." Jemma smiled at her nonplussed facial expression.

"They're just safeguarding them. Have you seen Brandon since you got here?"

"Only once. Our parents are keeping things traditional these last few days. That's why the men and women have suites on different floors, but we do talk to each other on the phone every day."

"I can't wait to see you in your dress tomorrow. Goodness, I still can't get over the idea that you're marrying Brandon," Jemma mentioned as the two of them settled on the bed to continue talking.

The TV was on *Lifetime*, but they weren't paying attention to the movie that was showing. The rain had decreased to a light drizzle, and per the meteorologist, it would be long gone before the wedding in three days. Sonya flushed at the words, and she let out a peaceful smile.

"Me neither, considering how I couldn't stand him in school."

Sonya recalled their fateful meeting years later with a heartfelt grin. After Jemma left Howard, Sonya had graduated but stayed to get her master's degree in communications and marketing. One day, Sonya's job flew her and a coworker to Baltimore to meet with a potential client. The meeting went well, and Sonya and Leo, her coworker, decided to go have a drink to celebrate. He had started getting all handsy at the restaurant and next thing Sonya knew, Brandon was there roughing the guy up. He happened to be there on a date, and he ended up walking her back to the hotel room. Brandon paid for a cab to take his date home, and she had been upset from being dismissed by him. Sonya and Brandon stayed up all night talking and catching up, which turned into a three-year relationship.

"I love that man so much, Jemma, I can't explain it." She let out a genuine grin at her best friend's words, blinking away the tears. Jemma had heard bits and pieces of how things progressed with Brandon over the years and was glad it had let to matrimony.

"Save all that mushy stuff for the wedding." Sonya threw a pillow at Jemma, who laughed.

"Honestly, I'm so happy for the both of you."

"Thank you, and I'm glad that you're here."

"Are you kidding? Your wedding got me away from the hospital for a much-needed break. Your dad paid half of the expenses; which I must thank him for. You're like a sister to me, and I wouldn't miss this for anything, but I am peeved at you for moving to Baltimore," Jemma told Sonya, who pouted.

"I'm sorry, hun, but I can always find a marketing job there. Brandon is the assistant physical therapist for the Ravens. I couldn't ask him to leave that."

"I understand. It gives me another place to travel to, but I already have my maid of honor/best friend pep talk ready for Brandon," she said, pushing up imaginary sleeves and flexing her forearms.

"You are a nut!" Sonya gasped once she got over her laughing spell.

WILL and Robert were sitting on the balcony of Will's room, enjoying the aftermath of the brief rainfall. Their reunion in the lobby was a jolly one as the brothers gave each other a good, long hug. The three friends had a filling dinner of steak and baby potatoes while they caught up on what was going on in their lives. After dinner, the two Rutherford men decided to keep the conversation going since they weren't done talking with each other yet.

"I'm going to kick your ass if you let another four months pass by and I don't see you," Will said to Robert, who grinned.

"Bro, I am a trained Marine. If anything, I would be the one doing the ass kicking," Robert countered, taking a swig of his beer.

They still favored each other, but his years of being on active duty for the Marine Corps had made Robert more aware, disciplined, and lethal.

"Oh sure. Throw that in my face," Will mumbled, rolling his eyes, and Robert smiled.

It was great to see Robert, and he felt good that his little brother was doing well. Robert lived in DC near the Pentagon, and he was a lieutenant in the intelligence sector. What did all that mean? Will had no idea since Rob couldn't go into detail about it.

"You're looking good, Will. Glad you're not letting the courtroom stress you out."

"That only comes when I'm working on a case, but I try not to let it get to me."

"You're going to love Chicago; it's a beautiful city," Robert said, stretching out his long legs.

"You've been there before?"

"A few times. Make sure you try the deep-dish pizza."

"Will do." They sat in silence, enjoying the breeze and calmness of the city.

"You have your speech ready?" Robert asked, looking at his brother.

"Yes. You OK with me being the best man?"

"Hell yeah! Dealing with wedding details, the bride, the bridesmaids... I'm good. Brandon told me you saw Jemma at the airport and that you both took the same flight in today," he said softly, glancing sideways at his older brother.

"She's the maid of honor. I almost popped him one for not telling me."

"How does she look?" Robert asked, studying Will.

One thing the military taught him was how to read people and their body language, and he was reading Will like the first edition of a literary classic.

"She looked..." What the hell was he supposed to say? Beautiful? Still sexy as hell? More gentle and softer? *Son of a bitch!*

"She looked OK... I guess."

Robert smiled and chuckled. "You are such a liar."

"OK, she looks gorgeous. She hasn't changed in all these years. If anything, there's a delicate nature to her now, but after what she did, I wouldn't touch her to shake her hand."

Robert shook his head at his brother's words. "I wish like hell you'd find out what went wrong ten years ago," Robert stated, and Will shook his head.

"It doesn't matter, Rob. She broke my heart and left me without as much as a phone call or letter. I'll be civil with her for the sake of the wedding, but I don't have anything to say to her."

"That's not right, Will. You clearly need closure on the matter, and maybe she does too. All I know is she was head over heels about you back in the day, and she wouldn't have left without reason provoking that action. Maybe all of this is happening so you can get answers. Just don't be too stubborn to seek them out."

Will was very surprised by Robert's words and how it seemed right coming from him. "When did you get so wise?" he asked as Robert stood up and stretched.

"It comes from my Jedi training."

"You're such a dork," Will said with a laugh as Robert waved before leaving the room.

Will stayed on the terrace for a few more minutes, thinking about his brother's words. Hell, maybe Robert was right. Perhaps if he closed that chapter in his life, he could move on, and his memories and dormant feelings for her could finally go away.

∼

JEMMA WAS LAUGHING at something Carla had said, and her smile faded when Brandon walked into the restaurant with his parents and groomsmen. The restaurant was adjacent to the hotel, and Sonya's father had reserved a table for the wedding party to meet before going their separate ways. Sonya rushed over to Brandon for a passionate but quick embrace, and the two sets of parents greeted each other. Will's gaze caught Jemma's just before he walked toward the breakfast buffet. She wiped her sweaty palms on her clothing. Her breathing came out in labored pants.

"Are you OK, Jemma? You're breathing funny," Carla commented with alarm, and she nodded.

"Yes, I'm fine. Thanks." The guys joined the table and introductions were made.

"So, I wanted everyone to meet so you can know who you're paired with for the ceremony. Will is with Jemma, Carla is walking with Robert, and Sandi is with Brandon's cousin Neil, who will meet them at the tux shop," Sonya announced, and she sat down to eat and talk to Brandon.

"Look at you, Jemma. You've grown into a beautiful woman," Robert said once he got to the table. She stood up to hug him with sincere glee on her face.

"Thank you, Robert. Look at how handsome you are. I know you're a heartbreaker," she claimed, looking over his good-looking, clean-shaven face.

"I would never break a lady's heart," he countered, and she laughed.

Will felt the sound tug at his heart and he took an intense, hefty breath. Will had watched her as she talked to Robert. He sat across from her seat, and Jemma returned to the table after her short conversation with Robert. Will glanced at her behind that was snug in her tailored shorts. She took a quick sip of her orange juice as they locked eyes again.

"Good morning," Jemma said, deciding to break the ice.

"Good morning," he answered over his coffee cup. She saw he had gathered a light breakfast of eggs, bacon, and toast.

"They have turkey bacon?" she asked since she knew he didn't eat pork.

"Yes. You didn't get any?"

"No. Per the bride, we're on food restrictions until the wedding," she replied, and he snickered at that. "All you ladies appear to be in okay shape to me. I'm sure you will look exquisite in your dress."

Jemma's heart skipped at his words. *He said "you" instead of you all... So, what? Stop reading too much into it!* Jemma mentally threw the book at her subconscious and looked around the table to see the other people engrossed in their own discussions.

"When did you grow that?" she asked, nodding toward his goatee.

"It's been a few years now. Why? You like it?" Will threw the question at her.

Before she could stop the words, they just tumbled out. "Yes, very much."

He looked at her, surprised that she answered truthfully, not noticing that Brandon, Sonya, and Robert were watching them.

"Thanks," he mumbled.

Will wasn't going to get sucked into having a simple dialogue with her just because they were sitting across from one another having breakfast. Jemma still didn't know how fate had allowed her to be less than five feet away from Will and she shook her head. She chuckled softly, covering her mouth with her hand.

"What's so funny?" he asked, pushing his cup away.

"I'm just finding it hard to believe that you're sitting here. That's all," she replied, their eyes slowing caressing each other's facial features.

"I know the feeling. It's like a dream."

"A dream or a nightmare?"

He sat there pondering the question. Will wanted to be mean and shout out that it was a hideous, terrifying hallucination, but he knew those wouldn't be true words. He was interrupted before he could say something, not sure if he wanted to answer or not.

"Let's go, ladies. We have a long day ahead of us," Yolanda, Sonya's mother, announced as she stood up. They got up to leave, and Jemma looked over her shoulder at Will. Her skin immediately tingled at the look he gave her.

∼

"Man, I look good!" Neil said, adjusting his vest and posing in front of a three-way mirror.

Will and Rob looked at each other and thought the same thing... *asshole*. Brandon's cousin was an "up and coming" music producer, and he made sure everyone knew it. He had apparently just flown in from L.A. from a business meeting with Tevin Campbell's people. Will knew bullshit when he heard it, and this guy was full of it. He flirted with the female associate at the tuxedo shop and was about to invite her to the reception before Brandon stepped in.

"Man, are you crazy? Don't invite people to my wedding, and we have a final head count!" Brandon said through clenched teeth, and Neil patted his back.

"Sorry, cuzzo. You're right; it's going to be plenty of single chicks there anyway. I can mack on them."

Brandon rolled his eyes and walked away. He couldn't stand his cousin and only had him in the wedding because his mom said it was the right thing to do. The guys were all in rented tuxedos except for the Rutherford brothers. They were wearing their own black Calvin Klein suits, and they just added the pale-yellow vests which matched the bridesmaids' dresses.

"OK, gentlemen, looking good," the store manager proclaimed, looking at each of them with a tape measure around his neck.

"What do you think, Dad?" Brandon asked his father, Elliot, who nodded with Sonya's dad, Ned, while he adjusted the sleeves. "Looks like you're ready to get married, son," Elliot answered, and Brandon nodded with confidence and support.

∼

Champagne was being passed around the bridal store in the private room that held Sonya's wedding members. Before she tried on her dress for the last time, the bridesmaids had done one last fitting, and she was pleased that no major alterations had to be made. Their dresses were long and satin with spaghetti straps; Jemma's dress was slightly different, and it was bunched under the bosom. The bridal store had a few customers in it, but that didn't take away from Senator Augustine's daughter being fully serviced. Everyone was in good spirits; the talking and laughing paused when Sonya came from the dressing room and turned around to model her dress with a big grin on her face. It was V-cut with three-quarter-inch lace sleeves and a delicate bead and pearl design on the bust and dress.

Yolanda teared up when she saw her daughter and Brandon's mom, Florence, dapped at her eyes. "My son is so lucky." Jemma's eyes watered at the beauty of Sonya's wedding dress and knew she was going to make a stunning bride.

"Brandon is going to want to skip the wedding and go right to the honeymoon when he sees you in that dress," Sandi said, and everyone laughed at that.

The wedding rehearsal started at two on Friday afternoon so that it would leave time to have dinner and enjoy the spa gathering that was planned for later. The ballroom where the ceremony and reception were to take place had already been decorated and awaited the festivities for tomorrow. The DJ had his space where he'd set up in the morning, and the tables were separated on the left and right sides by an aisle down in the center where the wedding party would walk down. A canopy altar draped in tulle and lace mixed with white lights, and yellow and white roses were setup up on the hardwood floor where Sonya and Brandon would speak their vows. The wedding color was pale yellow, and the tables had already been decorated with matching centerpieces. Sonya's yellow ranunculus, craspedia, and rose bouquet would be delivered tomorrow as well as the medium steamed white calla lilies flowers that the bridesmaids would carry.

The wedding planner, Amanda, was a short, feisty woman who was talking to the pastor, pointing toward the back of the room. The group was in the ballroom, waiting on Jemma and Sonya's parents to make an appearance. Will had on gray slacks and a matching Polo shirt. Everyone else was wearing formal attire for the day's activities, and the dinner was scheduled at a nice Mexican restaurant since Sonya and Brandon both loved the ethnic cuisine. Will and Robert were standing next to each other talking when Neil looked toward the door and let out a low whistle when Jemma walked in.

"Whoo! Look at that body!"

Will glanced, and he did a double take. She was wearing a coral wrap around dress that showed enough cleavage, and it stopped just above her knees with matching jewelry and low-heeled, slingback sandals to complete the outfit. Neil cleared his throat and raised his hand to his mouth to check if his breath was fresh.

"Let me go introduce myself." Neil started walking toward her, and Will grabbed his arm to stop him, his eyes shooting green fire.

"She's off limits to you."

"My bad, bro. That's you?"

"All day. Back off." He nodded and walked toward his aunt and uncle.

"You do know that you just claimed a woman you said you wouldn't touch to shake her hand, right?" Robert asked his brother with amusement.

"Shut it, Rob."

Will didn't care what he just did, but he didn't want that jackass anywhere near Jemma. She might be a heartless creature, but that didn't mean Will wanted that creep's hands on her. He didn't know where this surge of protection came from, but he wasn't about to chalk it up to anything than just a man looking out for a woman… just basic human actions. It had nothing to do with their past… absolutely nothing at all.

LATER THAT NIGHT, Jemma was sitting in the hotel bar too restless to sleep. The rehearsal had gone off without any problems, and the dinner had been a lovely time filled with laughs and good times. The spa outing was exactly what she needed, stress wise. The full body massage had felt so good, and the women had gotten their hands and feet done tonight so they wouldn't have to worry about it tomorrow. They had gotten a simple pedicure and just a clear polish after having their nails shaped and trimmed. She was sitting in a plush burgundy velvet cushioned booth that was crescent-shaped, and it was facing the windows. The vertical windows were open, letting in the cool breeze. Jemma was happy for her friend and was excited about the wedding, but she couldn't help but ponder where her love life was going... or not going. She had a busy career, but she didn't let it control her life. She was still in her twenties, and sometimes, she forgot that.

Jemma did go out but didn't like going to trendy clubs most people in her age group frequented. It had been so long since she had intercourse, and it was only so much she could do with a vibrator. Her mind kept wandering back to Will... about how good he looked, how wonderfully virile he smelled, and how assertive he was now. She was a little bit glad he was there. That way, she could admire him from afar and not have to talk to him since he obviously had some condescension toward her. Aside from the small talk at breakfast, they hadn't spoken to each other unless they had to, and that both bothered and was fine with Jemma. She took a sip of her beverage and placed the glass back down on the table.

"Since when do you drink?" a deep voice asked, and she closed her eyes briefly before looking up at Will.

"It's a virgin Cosmo," she answered him as he said down across from her.

His long fingers were wrapped around the short glass as he settled into the booth. He didn't know if she had come in before or after him, but after ordering at the bar, he had surveyed the room with its few occupants. He went to share her table when he saw Jemma sitting by herself after debating about it for a few minutes.

"Couldn't sleep?"

"Just restless. Wasn't ready for bed yet. What about you?"

"The same thing."

The waiter came and placed a plastic bowl of peanuts between them and walked away after they declined a refill on their cocktails. He took a swallow of his rum and Coke, their eyes connecting again like magnets. They couldn't seem to keep their eyes away from one another too long; as if looking away would cause the other to disappear. For some strange reason, Will felt at peace sitting here with her, and he tightened his hand around the glass at that thought.

"How was the bachelor party?" Jemma asked, crossing her legs and loosely interlocking her fingers together.

"It wasn't really a party... just a bunch of guys playing poker and talking shit in Mr. Drake's penthouse. Brandon isn't the strip club type of guy."

"Sounds like it was fun."

"Not for me. I lost eighty bucks." She let out an inward smile as another good draft flew in through the open windows.

"Do you have your speech ready?" Jemma asked, giddy that he was here having a simple, normal chat with her without any hate or contempt in his eyes and tone.

"Pretty much. I'm just going to speak from the heart." She nodded, gently biting her bottom lip, and Will felt a lurching in his belly at the act.

"You seem nervous that I'm sitting here," Will proclaimed, getting down to the nitty gritty.

"I am," she replied hoarsely.

"Why?"

"You really want me to answer that?"

"We'll come back to that. You haven't changed in all these years; you still look the same," Will's deep timbre voice was causing havoc on her senses as goosebumps appeared on her arms, which was weird because it was a warm night and she wasn't cold.

"Thank you. You're bulkier now, and the goatee looks really nice on you." He gave her a small grin, noticing they were fiddling with their drinks.

"How do you like being a nurse?"

"I love it. Been doing it for a few years now. What about you? Taking the law world by storm?"

He let out a dry chuckle at that. "You can say that. I made junior associate at Mac, Fry, and Greene."

"Really? That's great! Congratulations, Will." She inadvertently reached over to squeeze his hand, and the touch was like an exhilarating shock.

It was warm, sizzling, and powerful at the same time like it had spent the last ten years building and growing. He looked down at their touching skin, and they both pulled apart from one another.

"Thank you." He finished his drink and placed the empty goblet to the side.

"How does your girlfriend feel about you being a junior partner?" she asked him, her heart beating fast at the anticipated retort.

Will continued to stare at her, his gaze slowing roaming over the visible parts of her chest. He saw how small and dainty her hands were; his green sight going to her full, painted lips.

"I don't have a girlfriend, Jemma. Haven't had one in a long time."

His declaration caused a small part of her to be pleased with the news.

"What about you? Any jealous guys in the mix?"

"No," she whispered.

Being this close to the vixen was doing something wicked to his mojo. It had been months since he'd been with a woman, and his throbbing dick reminded him of that fact when he saw her lick her lips after taking the last swallow of her Cosmo.

"So, are we going to talk about the issue we've been avoiding?" Will came out and asked. Jemma cleared her throat and sat back, her hands trembling a little.

"There's nothing to discuss, Will," she replied in a firm voice, shaking her head.

"Like hell, it's not. I want to know why you left me back then," he said that last part with so much anger in his voice that she shuddered.

She glanced at the clock behind the bar, and it read 11:02 p.m. Jemma stood up and placed money on the table from her purse to cover both drinks.

"Just let it go, Will." She quickly left the bar and headed toward the bank of elevators.

The lobby was quiet, save for a few employees behind the desk and some people sitting on the lounging furniture, and she let out the air she was holding. She didn't want to discuss the past with Will, but he seemed determined to talk about it. She didn't know why it was so important to him and if she was able to leave it alone, then he should too. OK… she hadn't totally left it alone.

Those first two years after leaving Howard, all she could think about was Will and how things had gotten so bad between them, but she forced herself to get over it. Otherwise, it would have consumed her, and she couldn't let it keep its firm grip on her heart. She felt her skin burning and looked to the right to see Will stalking her. His eyes were blistering with raw emerald flames, and his footsteps carried him to her with a purpose.

Will grasped her forearm and bent down to speak in a low voice. "You're going to give me answers, damnit. I deserve them!" he growled in her ear.

Just then, a group of guests, who had gotten off the hotel trolley, walked toward the elevators just as the doors opened. Some people had shopping bags, souvenir goodies from tourist attractions and some were dressed like they'd just left the club. The cart became packed with Will standing at the back wall, and Jemma was standing in front of him. There were multiple conversations going on at once, and she tried to see if the button had been pushed for her floor. After realizing that it was going to stop on every floor, she let out a deep breath, wishing it would hurry up. Her nipples got hard when she felt Will's breath on her neck. *Right on her sweet spot!* It was hot, pleasant man breath, and she literally felt heavenly waves scurry down her body. Jemma gasped softly when he placed his left hand on her stomach and pulled her back to him.

Will closed his eyes and inhaled her scent. It was a womanly, light floral smell that went very well with her body harmony. He called himself every name in the book... idiot, fool, chump, but he didn't care. His body, heart, and mind were yelling three different things to him, but right then, his body was taking control. She felt the heat of his hand through her dress, and she welcomed the feeling it brought. Jemma thought he would let her go once a few people exited the elevator, but he started making up and down motions with his thumb across her belly button. His firm chest was pressed against her back, feeling the strong support behind her. Like his hand, it was hot, and she wanted to curl up against it like a cat. *Oh, how she missed this!* It wasn't the fact that it was a male, but that it was Will. Jemma missed his profound, woodsy aroma, his cozy warmth, wanted touch, and the way he looked at her like she was the only person in the room.

It seemed like both people groaned at the same time when he began to sway his hips side to side, which caused the impression of his penis to move to across the curve of her butt. While going through the wedding rehearsal, he couldn't stop himself from glancing at her rear end ever so often, and he could have sworn it had gotten bigger and plumper. He liked how the dress material stretched across the roundness so very much. Jemma couldn't seem to stop herself from slowly grinding her waist to match his movements. To the other passengers, it seemed like they were swaying to the soft music that was playing from the speakers. The area between her legs was beating like a jackhammer, and the encounter almost made her fall to her knees.

He enjoyed feeling each cheek rub over him, and he savored the sensation. Jemma wasn't the shy virgin when they'd first met. She was a full-fledged woman, and she knew exactly what she was doing. Jemma closed her eyes, imagining the rod that she felt with her butt. It had been too long for her to remember what it looked like, but she could feel the length and thickness of him. Will wrapped one hand around her pelvis and pushed her away from him before she made him bust a nut right there. She turned her head to look at him, and from the way his eyes were glowing and hearing his forced breaths, Jemma thought he was about to kiss her... and she wanted him to do it so very much.

The doors opened on her floor, and it took everything it had in Will to push her toward them. "Go."

She walked out on jellied legs and turned to look at him. The heavy breaths she was taking caused her breasts to expand against the cut of her dress, and he was distracted by the shape of them. Their eyes were speaking volumes that their bodies were responding to, and she stood there taking him in until the elevator doors closed.

PRECISELY NINE HOURS LATER, Jemma's hotel phone started ringing. She knew it was Sonya, and she let it ring a few more times before answering it.

"Yes?"

"I'm getting married today!" she screamed, and Jemma laughed.

"Yes, you are."

"C'mon and get your tush to my room. We're having breakfast, and I need you to do something for me." Sonya hung up, and Jemma moaned.

Her body was still wired from what happened in the elevator, and she had tossed and turned all night. The bride needed her, and she was at Sonya's beck and call for the day. Jemma took a hot shower and put on a pair of purple biker shorts with a matching shirt. After pinning up her hair with silver clips, she grabbed her bag with all her accessories and headed for Sonya's room. When she got there, the other bridesmaids were sitting on the couch, and the mothers were sipping tea at the table by the balcony doors. It was a beautiful, sunny day that promised to produce a warm breeze.

"Good morning, ladies." She received the same salutation and went to the bedroom where Sonya was at the desk writing a letter.

"Good morning, soon-to-be Mrs. Drake." Sonya smiled as she finished signing the letter.

"Morning. How did you—" Sonya paused when she saw how Jemma was looking with tired eyes.

"Rough night?"

"I didn't get much sleep, but I'll be OK after some coffee and food," Jemma reassured her, and Sonya nodded.

"Tell me what you want, and I'll order it. Can you take this letter to Brandon for me?" She gave Jemma a folded piece of paper and stood up.

"Am I waiting for a response?"

"If he wants to write one, sure. He's in room 1414."

Jemma gave Sonya her breakfast order and left the room, taking the stairs since it was one floor down. Finding the room, she knocked on the door and was surprised when it was opened by Will. He had on a black tank top with black and gray plaid pajama pants that were riding low on his hips. She almost dropped the paper when she saw a barbed wire tattoo going around his right forearm. *Oh my God! He is so damn fine!*

"Good morning, Jemma."

"G'morning," she managed to peep out.

Will stood like a statue as he eyed her body. He noticed that it really hadn't changed at all, especially her legs; they still looked good to him. Her shirt was fitted, and it was tight across her full breasts. Will was looking forward to seeing her all jazzed up. She was already beautiful, but with the fancy dress and makeup, he knew she would be stunning.

"Sonya asked me to deliver this to Brandon."

He opened the door further and peered at her butt as she walked past him. His head turned to follow her steps. Flashes of their elevator ride shot through his mind, and he cleared his throat. He had managed to get a few hours of sleep, but it didn't do any good because he had an erection throughout the entire night. The guys were in the suite watching the sports highlights on ESPN.

"Good morning, guys. Here, Brandon, this is from Sonya." He stood up and took the note, walking into the bedroom to read it.

There was a knock on the door, and Neil went to answer it. Will noticed that he had checked Jemma out when he walked past her. *I see I'm going to have to talk to this fool again.* Robert was looking at his brother and Jemma, noting that they kept staring at each other and looking away.

"That's a nice tat."

"Thanks. I got it about seven years ago," he replied, and she slowly nodded.

"Do you have any?"

"No."

"How did you sleep?" he asked, leaning against the wall.

"Off and on. You?"

"The same."

Will pushed off the wall and walked over to her with his arms folded. He lowered his head to her ear, and her skin began to crackle from his closeness. Her head inadvertently leaned toward him.

"We're going to finish our talk from last night," he informed her as Neil walked in with the room service cart.

"Tell Brandon I had to go." Jemma quickly left and headed back upstairs.

She wasn't prepared to see Will this early in the morning. It was too soon from last night, and she needed a longer buffer in between the sightings. Will watched her leave like a chicken and knew he was pacing himself. It was a lot going on today, but before they went their separate ways, he was going to get down to the bottom of what the hell happened ten years ago.

Hours later, the photographer had left Sonya's room and went back down to take more pictures of Brandon and the groomsmen getting ready. Afterward, he and his assistant went down to the ballroom to take more pre-wedding portraits. The hairstylist had come and gone, curling Sonya's hair with tight swirls and finishing it with a sparkling tiara.

The bridesmaids' hair was also curled, but their hair was draped over to one side and held back with a comb. They were all dressed and waiting on Sonya to make an appearance. Because Jemma was the maid of honor, she had a yellow orchard wrapped in her curls.

Amanda walked into the room with a clipboard in her hand dressed in a gold colored pants suit.

"Ladies, you look wonderful. Most of the guest have arrived. The DJ is playing mood music, and I need the bride so we can start making our way downstairs. It's twenty minutes to three o'clock." Amanda shot a quick look at her watch just as Sonya walked out her room with her mother and future in-law. With her makeup, jewelry, and hair completed, Sonya looked absolutely dazzling, and Jemma's eyes immediately began to water.

"Uh huh! Don't do that, Jemma," Sonya spoke, and she giggled.

"I'm sorry. You look amazing," Jemma said, hugging her friend. Sonya's cousin and Sandi agreed with nods of their heads.

They left the suite and headed toward the elevator, Jemma making sure she held on tight to the wedding band that was tied to her bouquet. People hooted and shouted out cheers as the bridal party walked through the lobby to get to the ballroom. The waterfall in the hotel garden had been reserved for the couple to take pictures after the ceremony, and Sonya was directed to a small room where she couldn't be seen.

A few minutes later, as more guests walked in, Brandon and his guys came down the hall. Jemma watched as he did the manly handshake with the fellas then walked into the room saying "hi" to individuals as he made his way to the pastor. Jemma's mouth got dry when she saw how fetching and stimulating Will looked in his tux. He was a fine piece of specimen with his neat haircut, trimmed facial hair, and polished shoes.

As he made his way to stand next to her, Will couldn't get over how different Jemma looked. She had transformed in a good way, and like he predicted, she looked unquestionably alluring. They were to be the last couple to walk before Sonya entered with her dad. Jemma knew she was there for her best friend, but it became a surreal dream when she walked down the aisle arm-in-arm with Will. He wondered if this was how their relationship would've ended if things worked out with him and Jemma. He had no doubt that they would've been married with a house full of kids. He knew it would be difficult walking alongside her, but he didn't expect for this onset of feelings to rush over him. Somehow, they had gotten through the ceremony with Jemma wiping her tears when the bride and groom expressed their commitment and love to each other with their vows.

Later, Will was watching Jemma from the bar as she and Robert were dancing to an Earth, Wind, and Fire song with other people. He absently thanked those who approached him about how good his speech was while everyone ate dinner. He couldn't keep his eyes off Jemma and how marvelous she looked all dolled up. Walking down the aisle and posing for pictures with her had almost been too much for him. Will was determined to get answers from her... tonight. Jemma smiled as Robert spun her around on the dance floor.

"You've got some moves, Robert." He smiled at that, spinning her again.

"So, when are you getting married?" she asked him.

"Oh, that's not happening anytime soon. I'm a busy bee." She grinned at that.

"I'm sure you are. What are your plans after the wedding?"

"I'm due back at the military base. What about you?"

"I have to be back at work on Tuesday. You know, Marines are the sexiest of all the armed forces." He laughed at her words.

"So, I've been told. Speaking of weddings, do I have to get my tux cleaned for you and big bro's?" She was shocked he had come out and asked that question.

"No. That ship has sailed," she responded in a serious voice, all playfulness erased from her face.

Robert looked at her with a crease in his forehead, not expecting her stern manner. "I find that hard to believe, especially since I've seen how you two have been looking at each other these last few days."

Jemma stopped dancing, and he became still too, seeing the anguish on her face. His eyebrows were drawn together in confusion when she shook her head.

"What happened, Jemma?"

"Did your brother send you to ask me?" she countered sardonically. People continued to dance around them, not paying attention to the stationary duo on the floor.

"First of all, my brother doesn't send me to do anything. Second, I'm asking as a friend. If you need to talk, I'm here to listen," Robert let her know, and she trembled.

Maybe she should talk to Robert. It might do her some good to get everything out in the open and to help with the healing process. "Promise me you won't tell Will."

"I can't do that, Jemma. We don't keep secrets from each other, but I can promise to keep an open mind with whatever you tell me." Will looked on with interest as he saw Jemma and Robert exit the room together. *Where are they going?*

JEMMA SAW various reactions pass across Robert's face as she told him what had happened. She was leaning against the wall, and Robert was pacing in front of her.

"So, I packed my things, transferred to Illinois State, and moved back to Chicago after graduating."

"Son of a bitch! I can't believe my grandmother did that. So that's why she drugged Will," he said to himself.

"What are you talking about?"

"Felicia slipped Will a large dose of ecstasy, and she almost caused him to overdose. I rushed him to the hospital and stayed with him that night. That's why we were trying so hard to find Felicia… to find out why she drugged Will."

Jemma's heart raced at that information. She hadn't known that had happened, and she was glad Robert had taken Will to seek medical treatment. She had seen first-hand that some people didn't recover from an overdose. Her hands grew clammy at the realization that Will had almost died.

"Did you ever find out why she did it?" Jemma's question came out hoarsely, and he shook his head at her.

"She never said a word. A few days after she was arrested, her bond was paid. I'm willing to bet my military career that Granny paid the bill. Damn, Jemma. I'm sorry about all of this."

"It's not your fault, Robert." She shrugged, looking toward the ballroom.

"You have to tell Will." Her eyes got large at his words.

"No, I can't!"

"Why not? He needs to know what happened. He's a victim in this like you were. If you don't, I will."

"Robert, I—"

"Just listen to me for a minute. You opened my brother's heart, and I know that he loved you very much. He was talking about spending the rest of his life with you. I know you genuinely cared for and loved Will. I'm sorry as hell for what my grandmother did to break up what you guys had. You two should talk and get everything out in the open. I don't know about you, but Will has never gotten over you. He doesn't want to admit it because he has his male pride, and he's stubborn as hell."

Jemma blinked back the tears that were threatening to fall. She knew Robert was right, but she was scared to talk about what happened. She didn't want to feel vulnerable with her feelings for Will again. Again, she wished things had turned out different.

"I haven't gotten over him, either," she said in a soft, teary voice.

"Talk to him. I'll give you a week to tell Will."

She nodded and went to the bathroom to freshen her face. She dabbed a cold paper towel over her eyes and let out a deep breath. She felt like a big stone had been lifted off her chest and she knew Robert was right; Will did deserve to know what his grandmother had done. Jemma probably should've said something back then, but there was Mona, Felicia, her out-of-control emotions, his hospitalization—all those factors were present and had gotten in the way of them communicating. She didn't want to have the same draining conversation with him, so she decided to write a letter and would give it to Will before he left. Was that a weak cop-out? It probably was, but that was the best solution she could come up with. She walked back to the reception just in time to see Sonya throw the bouquet, and it was caught by one of Brandon's family members. She looked around and didn't see Will anywhere.

She stayed at the wedding until the newlyweds left for their honeymoon to Cabo San Lucas. As she rode the elevator to her floor, Jemma smiled as she recapped the day. She sincerely wished Sonya and Brandon a long and happy marriage. She was glad she hadn't run into Will on her way to her room; she didn't want to confront him right then. She was looking forward to relaxing the rest of the night in that queen size bed in her room. Even though the married couple had left, the reception was still going on; it wasn't scheduled to be over for another two hours, but Jemma was partied out. Stepping off the elevator, she sniffed the flowers from her bouquet as she walked down the hall. Jemma stopped suddenly when she saw Will leaning against the wall across from her room. He had his hands in his pockets with his ankles crossed. His tuxedo jacket was open, revealing the yellow vest.

"What are you doing here?" she asked, butterflies jumping around in her stomach.

"Figured I'd meet you on your turf, so you won't disappear on me again. We're going to have our talk right now."

She nodded, giving him the one-minute sign. Jemma opened the door with the keycard, placed the flowers in the fridge, and slipped out of her heels. She walked out the room, using the door stopper to keep it cracked. They stared at each other in silence for a few moments. Will closed his eyes when her perfume fragrance snuck up on him. She was shorter without her shoes, and he almost forgot how petite she was.

"You have fun at the wedding?" she asked

He nodded.

"You?"

"Yes. I saw you and Robert leave the reception," Will said in a no-nonsense tone, and she raised her chin at the sound.

"Yes, we did. What do we need to talk about?"

"Ten years ago, why did you leave me? Was it another guy?"

"No!" She was taken aback at his words. *How could he think that?*

"Were you bored with me?"

"No."

"Did you fall out of love with me?"

"No, Will. That's not it." She didn't say anything to him, and his eyebrows jumped up in anticipation.

"I'm waiting for an answer, Jemma."

"It was your grandmother!" she yelled.

"What the hell are you talking about?"

"The day after that fundraiser, she showed up at my place with a check to get out of your life. When I tore it up, she showed me a picture of you and Felicia kissing. Your hands were all over her."

Her voice shook at the last part, but she didn't falter. Will took a deep breath to calm his anger and racing heart. He should've known his grandmother had something to do with what happened. Mona never liked Jemma, but he honestly didn't think she would go to that extreme. The pieces were falling into place now that he thought about it. The whole thing had been staged by Mona and Felicia. He hadn't known about the check or the photograph. Needless to say, he was pissed at both Jemma and his grandmother.

"Robert told me that Felicia almost caused you to overdose. I-I didn't know about that," she said softly.

His restraint snapped at that, and he couldn't stop himself from having an attitude. "Yeah? Well, had you stayed and talked to me, you would've known!" he replied to her angrily. His hands balled up into fists at his side.

She looked at him with harshness in her eyes as they blazed with fury. Jemma stormed over to him, poking him in his chest repeatedly with each word.

"Excuse you! I called you several times, went by your apartment. You're the one who ran off to find Felicia when I tried talking to you."

"Because I was trying to figure out why the hell she drugged me! You of all people should have known that picture was fake. I didn't have any interest in Felicia. I loved you, Jemma, only you."

Tears fell down her face as she turned away from Will to go inside her room. The meddling of two people had caused them to lose several years of being together. Will hated the fact that she didn't trust him and allowed outsiders to ruin their relationship. But to be fair to her, they both had been duped, and it was sickening that his family member was responsible for it. He reached out to clutch her arm and pulled her around to face him. He cupped her cheek and lowered his head to kiss her. It wasn't a simple peck either; Will *consumed* her with his lips, and she returned the gesture with eagerness. It felt like a tremendous homecoming when their lips linked. It was a combination of the feel of rain on a hot day, the first bite of a fresh peach, and the first smell of a freshly bloomed rose. Will wiped her tears away with his thumbs as he deepened the kiss. It felt so good for both people to taste each other again.

They hungrily continued the smooching; neither caring that they were in the hallway for anyone to see them. Jemma moaned as she wrapped her arms around his waist from inside his open jacket, her body awakening from this physical interaction. To Will, she tasted a thousand times better than he remembered. To feel her tongue caressing his, to savor her lips and tongue… Her flavor after ten years was pure heaven. She didn't know that he had walked them back into the room until she heard the door close. He released her lips. His eyes caught hers again, and her eyelashes were spikey from her tears.

"Will, I—"

"Ssh… We'll talk later," he told her gently.

Jemma nodded, standing on her tiptoes to kiss him again. They stood in the middle of the room and were content with just kissing each other. Unlike the first one, this one was easy and tender. The lushness of her bottom lip was doing things to him and causing his blood to boil. Her hands had gripped the lapels of his jacket, and she felt the zipper of her dress being pulled down its track. The cold air from the AC felt good against her overheated skin. While still kissing him, she slipped out her dress, and calmness was tossed out the window as she tugged at his clothes to help get rid of them. Will stepped back and took in the yellow strapless bra and matching thong. Gone were the girly curves of her college years. She was now a goddess and he liked what he saw; her voluptuous breasts, flat tummy, shapely thighs, and smooth legs. He moved to glance at her booty and slapped the globe of her butt.

"Damn," he murmured, and she grinned.

Will walked to the door and placed the *Do Not Disturb* placard on the knob and locked it. Since she had already removed his vest and shirt after undoing them, he unbuttoned his pants, and they fell down his muscular legs. Will's chest was hairless, toned, and had the perfect six-pack. She was looking forward to running her hands and mouth over the firm torso. Jemma knew Will had taken his time to inspect her body, so it was her turn. Lowering her eyes, she ran them down his thighs to his hairy legs. What she wanted, missed, and couldn't keep her eyes off was his thick erection pushing against the black boxers. Her mouth parted when he removed the barrier, his manhood jutting from the bushy patch at the junction of his legs. It looked bigger and thicker, and she was throbbing something fierce in her core, her hard nipples pushing against her bra. Will stepped in front of her and reached up to run his finger over her bottom lip.

"I want to go slow... to take my time, Jemma, but I can't. I know I can't."

"It's OK. I don't want you to."

He bent down to kiss her again as his thumbs hooked under the elastic band of her thong to push it down her legs. He picked her up with ease, and she willingly wrapped her legs around him. Taking them to the bed, he got on top of her and removed her bra. Jemma gasped and sighed at the same time when Will closed his lips around her left nipple. His mouth felt warm over her cool skin and between the licking and suckling, she was about to shatter, feeling the other big hand tending to her other breast. He hadn't tasted anything this sweet in years. He lapped at her, gently biting the hardness. She didn't have time to think when he shoved her legs apart and lowered his head to her pulsating center. Jemma hadn't had the chance to turn on any lights, the only illumination came from the outside through the open curtains.

Will nibbled and nipped the flesh of her inner legs until he got to the area he craved. She arched her back, and a high pitch moan escaped from her open, wet mouth when he started to lap at her with the tip of his tongue. Nothing felt so perfect or as good as that. She cupped his head, and her body began to quiver against her resolve. After a few slow laps of his tongue from the tip to the flat surface, she came apart from a mind-blowing and overdue orgasm. Elated tears ran down her face at the sensation, her free hand clutching the comforter in a strong grip. Will hooked her legs to keep her from moving away... He still had some more tasting to do. Jemma forgot how good he was at this. His hands were roaming all over her body... her thighs, stomach, legs, and breasts. She braced herself on her elbows and tossed her head back in pleasure.

He held her legs apart as she had another climax, her entire body rocking from the release. Will was hard as marble, and after giving her a soft kiss on her outer lips, he scuttled up her body. She licked her lips as he used his hand to guide himself inside her. Jemma gasped and convulsed as he slowly entered to the hilt.

"Fuck," he whispered when her flesh molded around him.

God help him, he wanted to go slow and felt they needed it to last, but once he got inside her tight, succulent goodness, he lost all determination. With powerful, deep strokes, he moved in and out of her honied center. She moaned with bliss at each drive, her nails raking down his chiseled back.

She caught his gaze as he pumped inside her, and she arched up to kiss him. Will did everything in his power to not come so soon, but once her inner muscles latched onto him, it was over after that. He knew she had had a third orgasm, and that made his climax intense and monumental. He collapsed on top of her, and she wrapped her arms around him, their sweaty foreheads resting against one another. Will's body was literally prickly, and he didn't know what to make of it. He rolled off her a few minutes later, and they both were staring at the ceiling, trying to catch their breath.

"You were tight, Jemma," he said in a hoarse, croaky voice, and she knew he could use some water.

She turned her head to look at him, still on a high from the multiple orgasms. "What do you mean?"

"I mean, you're tight as hell down there. Haven't you been with anyone in ten years?" Jemma let out a deep breath before answering.

"I was busy with nursing school, and I didn't have the time. I did date this one guy, but that didn't count because the sex was over very fast and let me say, you are really killing the mood with your question." The words had just slipped from her mouth when he leaned toward her and gave her a caring kiss. She sighed and licked her swollen mouth when he pulled back.

"Come here." Will tugged at her so she could lay on his chest.

She heard the solid beating of his heart and smiled softly when he wrapped the blanket around them. "I missed you, Will," she admitted, her hand over his heart.

"I've missed you more," he replied, running his hand through her messy hair.

"What about you?" she asked seconds later, enjoying the cozy setting with him, lifting her head to glance at him.

"As far as what?"

"You being with someone else?" He paused at her question, not knowing how she'd handle the truth. No, he hadn't been celibate all these years, but the few women he had slept with had been one-night stands.

"There have been other women, but it was just sex. It didn't mean anything, Jemma. I wasn't in a relationship with them nor did I love them," he explained while keeping eye contact with her, and she nodded.

Jemma got quiet as she contemplated Will's news. She hadn't expected him to be a monk while they were apart, but a tiny part of her was jealous. Will knew she was pondering what he had just told her, and he was thinking about what she'd said in return. If Jemma said her past relationship didn't mean anything, then he believed her. Still, one and a half guy in ten years was a damn good thing.

"When do you plan on checking out?" Will asked, breaking into Jemma's thoughts.

"Monday morning. I don't have to be back at work until Tuesday, and I wanted to go do some sight-seeing tomorrow. What about you?"

"I was going to check out tomorrow morning, but since the rooms are paid through the weekend, I could stay an extra day. Would you be terribly disappointed if you didn't get to go out tomorrow?" he asked as he shifted her to sit astride him, his private part standing at attention.

"And why wouldn't I get the chance to do that?" she asked with a gasp when he reached up to tweak her nipples.

"Because I want to lay up in this room all day buried between your legs."

And on that note, round two started for them that ended up leading to three more bouts of raging sex.

~

JEMMA LET out a profound breath as she stood in the big shower. It had three shower heads at different angles with powerful streams. She had two going with her hair pinned up to prevent it from getting wet. The events from the previous night flashed through her mind like an erotic montage. She recalled each moment Will kissed, bit, licked, and lapped her body. She nearly wept at how gentle he was at one time and couldn't contain her eagerness when he got rough and aggressive the next moment. She had long since washed herself but was enjoying the hot water. Jemma's heart began to race when she heard the door open and Will got in. She looked to see him turn on the other shower head and inclined back to let the water flow over his head. Her eyes slowly ran down his fantastic body, and she tongued her upper lip as she remembered how she ran her mouth over his tasty skin.

"You keep looking at me like that, and you're going to get it." His deep words caused her to snap out her reverie, and she smirked. She smelled a burst of manly body wash that had the scent of oak and citrus, and she faced him, watching as he lathered his arms.

"That smells good."

"Thanks. I went to my room to get a few things."

"You just made yourself comfortable in here, I see," she commented, and he grinned.

"Do you mind?"

"No."

"Good. Come wash my back for me, please?"

She took the towel and began to wash his solid back in small strokes. Will liked how her fingers scraped his skin and how her hands slid down his sides. His head turned; their eyes met in a silent wanting. She stepped closer to him, her soapy hands moving to his front area. Will didn't say anything when Jemma placed her lips on his back, lowering her hands to his stomach. He felt her nipples stabbing against his back, his eyes sliding down when he felt her hands start to fondle his hard dick. Between the hot water, steam and her slick hands, it was causing his senses to go on overload. He braced his hands on the wall and the shower door while enjoying her caress. He felt her erratic breathing as she stepped on her tippy toes to gnaw at his shoulder blade.

"Mmm...that feels so good," he rumbled in a gruff voice that came out in pants.

"It sure does," Jemma agreed as she was twisting her hands while rubbing his engorged prick.

Will's harsh sighs were turning her on, and she was displaying a satisfied smile when he let out a huge load in her hands. Jemma wanted him between her legs so bad. She was about to beg for it, but her phone rang. She cursed under her breath as she stepped out the warm spray.

"Don't go," Will said to her, hanging onto her fingers.

"I'll be right back."

Wrapping a fluffy towel around her, Jemma got to the phone on the fifth ring and picked up.

"Hello?"

"Hey, it's Sandi."

"Oh, hi. What's up?"

"Carla and I are going to go shopping. You want to join us?" Jemma smiled at the invite, knowing she was going to decline since she wanted to spend as much time with Will as she could.

"Thank you for the offer, but I'm going to just chill in my room. It's been a long weekend," she answered, glancing out the hotel windows to see that it was windy outside.

"Okay, maybe we can go for drinks later."

"Yeah, maybe. Have fun today."

They disconnected, and Jemma hit the button to order room service. After replacing the handset, she applied her jasmine scented lotion on her body and tied the towel again. She went to the balcony door and stared at the clouds. Will came out with a towel around his middle and wrapped his arms around her waist from behind.

"Who was on the phone?" he asked, sniffing her neck.

"Sandi. She invited me to go shopping with her and Carla."

"You didn't want to go?"

"No. I want to spend my time with you," she returned truthfully, and he was stunned by her answer; as if this was their last time seeing each other.

"We're going to see each other after this, Jemma."

"How? You live in D.C., and I'm in Chicago."

He turned her to face him, his hands interlocking with hers. He decided not to tell her that he had moved to Chicago. Not to deceive her, but because they had other pressing matters to talk about.

"Trust me, we'll see each other again." Jemma looked into his eyes, and she knew she could believe what he'd said.

"I ordered room service," she mentioned as he undid the knot of the towel.

"Oh good. I'm starving." Will kissed her slow and steady as their tongues went back and forth, fondling each other.

Will lifted Jemma onto the table by the balcony, and he stepped between her thighs. She wrapped her legs around him, tugging at the towel that did nothing to hide his hard-on. Jemma gasped softly as his big hands slid down her body at a slow pace, his left hand creeping toward her drenched clit. He slid two fingers inside her warmth, his thick extremities penetrating her deeply. She opened her legs wider and started to grind herself against the long digits. It was a temporary solution until Will could give her the good stuff, but she liked this as well. He bowed down to greedily take a stiff nipple into his mouth and licked it as he increased his hand motions. There was a knock on the door, but they had more important things going on than to worry about an interruption. Will rasped in her ear he wasn't stopping for anything as he slid his rod inside her, and they made good use of the sturdy hotel table. The next day, Jemma drowsily woke up and looked over her shoulder, expecting to see Will, but all she saw was a note laying in the indentation of the pillow.

Holding the sheet over her naked chest, she reached for the paper, her heart slamming at the words.

This isn't over between us. Went to take care of unfinished business. I'll be in contact – Will.

She closed her eyes and lay back on the bed. Will had surely made up for her lengthy abstinence, and she already wanted some more. Jemma was curious by Will's note but didn't dwell on it because her inquiries couldn't be answered right now. This was the best weekend she had had in a long time, and she was already missing him. She wondered how Will was going to get in contact with her since she hadn't given him her phone number or address. Jemma got out the bed after lying there, thinking about Will and headed toward the bathroom.

∼

WILL WALKED toward the sitting room of his grandparents'... well... his grandmother's house. After they got divorced years ago, Joshua kept his word and let Mona keep the house. It hadn't changed much, and he was hoping to keep this trip short and informative. After checking out of the hotel, he had changed his ticket to fly back to D.C. before heading to his new residential city. He wanted to do nothing but stay in bed with Jemma since he hadn't gotten his fill of her, but he had to see his grandmother to get confirmation. Mona had aged well over the years, even though she was now walking with a cane.

"Will! This is such a nice surprise. What brings you here? Would you like something to drink?" He watched her put down the book she was reading, and he sat down on the settee across from her.

"Jemma Alden. What did you do a decade ago?" he inquired, getting right down to business.

Mona's nose flared, and she rolled her eyes. "Why in the hell are you asking about her?"

Will's eyebrows shot up in disbelief. He'd never heard his grandmother curse before and wondered why she was so upset.

"Tsk tsk. Such language, Grams. I ran into Jemma at a wedding, and we got to talking. You tried to bribe her to get out of my life?"

"Yes, I did. That little fool tore up a fifty-thousand-dollar check. Who does that?" Will shook his head at that and pinched his lips.

"Someone who loved me. What did you do?"

"All I did was show her a picture of you and Felicia Childress. What difference does it make?"

"You cost us ten years from being together. That's what difference it makes!" Will shouted, standing up and paced the room.

"Will, I—"

"Let me tell you something. You're done with being deceitful and manipulating things. She's back in my life, and she is not going anywhere this time," he announced and headed toward the door. Will paused outside the room and looked at her.

"It's sad, Grandmother. After everything you've said and done, you still ended up alone. I'm not going to be like you."

Will left with those words, and Mona watched him depart, considering what he said.

∼

JEMMA WALKED into her apartment in Hyde Park, glad to be back home where she could sleep in her own bed. She left the luggage by the door and removed her shoes. On the cab ride to the airport and on the flight back home, she thought about everything that had gone down in Atlanta. She hadn't expected to see Will but was glad he was there because they were finally able to find out what happened to cause them to break up. They didn't converse about what would happen going forward, but she guessed they'd cross that bridge when they got to it. To be honest, he had her feeling old and new emotions, and she didn't know how to process them. Walking to her bedroom, she grabbed the wireless phone and dialed a familiar number.

"Hey, Jem."

"Hi, Auntie. What's going on?"

"Nothing much. Just watching TV. Stan and I went and got some things for the yard earlier, and we've been planting all day." Jemma smiled at that, knowing Stan was more into gardening than Paris was.

"That sounds like a stress-free activity."

"I enjoyed it. How was the wedding?" Jemma answered the question as she walked into her long closet and sat down to dig under some empty shoe boxes.

"That's good. I hope they got our gift."

"I'm sure they did," she commented, pulling out an orange shoe box and placed it next to her.

"What's wrong, Jem? I'm getting a vibe from you."

She sighed and sat back against the wall with her legs stretched out. "He was at the wedding."

"The President?" Paris asked with a gasp, and Jemma frowned with a laugh.

"What? No. Why would you say that?"

"You said Sonya's dad is a Senator; I thought maybe the president would've attended the wedding."

"No, Auntie, you are so off base. Are you and Stan reliving the hippie days and smoking those left-handed cigarettes again?" Paris smiled, thinking about the time when Jemma caught them smoking pot.

"No, not recently. Although that does sound fun for tonight…"

Jemma rolled her eyes and squeezed the bridge of her nose. "Aunt Paris…"

"Sorry. Who was at the wedding?"

"Will"

"Will?" Paris gulped, sitting up on the couch. "Not *your* Will from school!"

"Yep."

"Shut the front door!"

"I know."

"Well, what happened? Don't leave anything out!" Jemma omitted some details as she told her aunt a few things, but not everything. Paris didn't need to know that Will had given her numerous, mind-blowing orgasms.

"That old geezer! If I ever see that old woman, I'm slapping her sideways."

"You're not a violent person, Auntie."

"Well, she deserves it. Are you OK?"

"Yes and no. We talked, but things are still out in the open."

"I know you must be going through a lot right now, but don't overthink it and just talk to him whenever Will contacts you again," Paris stated when Stan came in and sat next to her on the couch. He had picked up her feet and placed them on his thighs.

"Do you want to get back together with him?"

"Is that even an option for us after all this time?"

They talked for a few more minutes, and they hung up with Paris letting Jemma know she'd tell Stan hi for her. Jemma put the receiver down and opened the shoe box. It was filled with souvenirs from her time with Will from college. It contained Polaroids, the stuffed animal he had won for her that summer she'd spent in North Carolina and notes they had written to each other. She stared at the pictures of their younger selves—in love and happy. She lay down in the closet and continued to stare at the pictures with a tranquil grin on her face. The memories kept her company in the quiet space.

CHAPTER 2

It was Tuesday afternoon, and Jemma had just finished applying a cast to the right arm of a thirteen-year-old teenage boy who had decided to play WWF with his friends.

"This green cast is cool," the boy snickered, and his mother popped him upside his head, causing Jemma to shake her head.

"Just make sure he stays off the roof. Here are a sling and a prescription for painkillers from the doctor."

Jemma told the patient's mother as she handed her the discharge paperwork. Jemma filed his chart after he left and sighed. She had been at work since eight that morning, and the ER was busy as ever. Most were glad to see her back, and in a way, she was eager for the distractions since they were keeping her mind off Will. Clocking out for lunch, she headed toward the café where her co-workers were waiting for her. Walking into the state-of-the-art cafeteria, she saw that it was half full. It could hold over a hundred people, and it was open 24/7. After getting her food, she headed toward their usual window table, smiling when she saw the two people. Phoebe was a tall, redheaded Caucasian woman who was married to a detective.

"Hey, guys."

"Jemma, will you please tell Phoebe she needs me to go shopping with her?" Gary said as soon as she sat down.

"You might want to consider it. He did stop you from buying those blue leather pants," Jemma countered, opening her water bottle.

"They were cute!" she exclaimed, and Gary shook his head. Jemma reached to grab from his nachos, and Gary swiped at her hand.

"So, how was the wedding? Where are the pictures?" Phoebe asked Jemma, bouncing in her seat.

"It was great and beautiful. I'll show you when I get some from Sonya."

"Did you heed my suggestion?" Gary asked Jemma, as she was taking a bite of her lettuce wrap. His idea had been the last thing on her mind, but she technically did hook up with a groomsman.

"Umm... yes and no," she mumbled around a mouthful of food.

"What suggestion? What's going on?"

"I told Jemma she needed to get laid at the wedding," he answered Phoebe's question, and the other girl nodded.

"Oh, I agree with that. If I don't get some at least four times a week from Logan, I'd go crazy. I don't see how you went this long without sex." Jemma rolled her eyes and ate some of her tortilla chips.

"So, what's this yes or no answer?" She broke down the story, leaving out a key few details.

"Wow!"

"Was it worth it?"

"Oh, God, yes! Very much so."

"We need to drink to that!" Gary replied, raising his juice bottle, and the two girls laughed at that.

The rest of the day passed uneventful, and Jemma wondered how Will was doing as she drove home later that night.

~

"You know you have a meeting in ten minutes?" Fiona reminded Will as she walked into his office a week later.

He was leaning against the window, looking out at the bustling activities on Michigan Avenue. For it to be a Monday morning, the street was busy with people and vehicles. He admitted that the commotion put him at ease, and he knew that Jemma was somewhere within the city limits. He could see the lake from his window and saw scattered boats on the clear, choppy water. Will wore a gray suit with a black shirt and matching tie.

"Yes, I know, Fiona."

"It's your first partners' meeting. I need you to pep up. You drank all the coffee I made, so you should be springing off the walls." He grinned and turned to look at her.

"I'm good. Thanks for setting up the office."

She had arranged the desk and computer the way he liked it and had carefully placed his paintings and plants where they best complimented his spacious office. He liked that the windows offered better lighting and that he could space things out in the workplace. The office was located in a twenty-story building that housed other businesses like a doctor's office, an accounting firm, and a foster care agency.

"You're welcome, Will."

There was a knock on the door, and Dante Fry walked in. He was an older African-American lawyer and one of the senior partners in the firm. He had been instrumental in Will's placement in the company given his close friendship with Mr. Sachs, Will's mentor and law professor from college.

"How do you like the office?"

"It's great. Thank you, Mr. Fry." Dante had told Will several times to call him by his first name, but he never did out of respect.

"You ready to go?"

"Yes, sir."

Will grabbed his leather notebook, and Fiona gave him a supportive grin. In the glass-encased conference room, Will and two other junior associates along with the other senior partner sat around the big, glossy oval table.

"Good morning. Let's open the meeting by first welcoming our new addition to the firm, William Rutherford. I hope everyone was able to read the memo and look at his track record and acknowledgments in and out the courtroom," Dante said. Then, he let Will have the floor to thank them for the opportunity to work with such a great establishment.

"OK, now to get down to business. I know you have been following the news of Michael Vy. He was the second-round rookie pick by the Chicago Bulls last year. He had a fantastic first year, but he was recently charged with first-degree murder of his girlfriend. He has since been dropped from the team and lost half of his endorsements. Now we're representing him," the head of the law firm, Shane Greene informed the people in the room, while Will was taking notes.

"Rutherford, you're lead chair." Will looked up at him, astonished by the declaration.

A white attorney who was on his way, or so he thought, to becoming a partner named Mickey Thorpe sat up in objection. He had worked there for over three years, and he was sick and tired of these young hot shots coming in taking his cases and trying to push him out the door.

"Excuse me, Shane. I know you're trying to do what's best for the client, but this is an extremely high-profile case. I think a more experienced attorney should take the reins on this case. I'd be more than willing to offer my services." Shane and Dante looked at each other, and Will noticed the movement.

"Well, Mickey, no one had any objections when you were first hired, and you were the lead on that physician poison case. All new junior associates get big cases to see what they're made of and how they conduct themselves. Will can handle this, Mickey. Rutherford, you've been assigned a paralegal to assist you, and we're here to help if you need us," Shane said to Will, who nodded.

Will's eyes shot over to Mikey, who he didn't like. The fact that his first case with the new company was a huge one and a co-worker doubted him added to his adrenaline to kick ass on the case.

"Is Mr. Vy still in lockup?"

"Yes, he's in the county. Apparently, his parents didn't like the first lawyer, so they came to us on a friend's recommendation. Any more questions?"

"No, Mr. Greene."

"Good."

They went over a few more cases being assigned, and the meeting was over. When Will got back to his office, he unbuttoned his jacket and pulled up directions on how to get to the jail from his location on the computer. Dante came into his office a few minutes later, and Will looked at him. Will knew he was a good man and welcomed any advice he'd dish out.

"You OK with this?"

"Are you kidding? Cases like these are what I live for."

"If you need anything, just let me know. You're still young; don't get burned out before you even begin. And don't worry about Mickey. He feels like he should have all the big projects."

"He didn't faze me. Thanks for your offer."

"A bunch of us are going out for dinner and drinks Friday night after work. You should come. One more thing, you won't get to meet the other partner, Morris Mac for a few weeks. He's on vacation with his wife, and they went to Europe," Dante let him know. Will made sure to tell his secretary, so she could put the dinner on his calendar.

After Dante left, Fiona buzzed into his office. "Mr. Rutherford, Kelly Meadows is here to see you."

After knocking on the door, the paralegal came into the office and stood at the door with a notebook clasped tightly in her hands.

"Mr. Rutherford, I'm Kelly Meadows. It's nice to meet you."

"Same here."

She was dressed in a brown pants suit with a white shirt and heels. He stood up and went to go greet the medium height, black woman with a permed hairdo and thin-rimmed glasses. She was a small, mousy woman and kept her eyes downcast.

"So, tell me something about yourself," Will said, as they sat on the two-seater couch in the office.

"I'm twenty-four. I started out as a court reporter and later took courses to become a paralegal. I've been here for about two years," she explained in a low voice.

"You ever work on any high-profile cases?"

"Just one, Mr. Rutherford."

"OK, let's get started. First thing, please call me Will, and second, I need to go see Mr. Vy today. I hope you're prepared to work long hours on this case, Miss. Meadows."

Kelly nodded and opened her notebook while pushing her glasses up. She had heard that this case was a biggie for the firm, and they needed a good outcome.

∼

JEMMA USUALLY WASN'T A DRINKER, but she was sorely tempted to order another glass of Merlot. She sighed at her blind date that Gary had set up for her, trying to stay engaged in his conversation. She'd completely forgotten about it until he reminded her earlier that day. She didn't want to go given what had happened with Will in Atlanta, but she hadn't heard from him, and she'd promised Gary. Her date was a friend of a friend of Gary's, and he was so boring. It was Friday night, and she was tired. Jemma had rushed home after working eleven hours to change for her date, but the guy was so dull, she wished she would've stayed home.

"So, you see, people have misunderstood the Loch Ness monster for years. If they just read the books, the truth will be known," Zach pointed out, and she sighed again, wishing the waiter would come back so she could order that wine.

"I understand, Zach," she told him, sitting back in the cushioned chair. She really didn't, but she hoped that would end the topic. Zach was a short, light-skinned man with a bald head and a crooked nose that looked like it had been broken more than once.

"I've searched high and low for authentic photos of Nessie." She slowly nodded her head, looking around Del Prado's.

It was a nice, snazzy new restaurant in the south loop area. It was her first time there, and she liked it… even if her date was mind-numbing as hell. They had been seated fifteen minutes ago, and they had gotten their drinks while waiting for the appetizers. *Is he still talking about that freakin' monster?* Jemma's skin started to tickle, and her nipples turned into hard pebbles. She knew her body was reacting to Will being near, but that was ridiculous since he wasn't here. She wore a white skin-tight V-shaped halter dress that snapped at the back of her neck with red accessories that included high-heeled shoes and red jewelry. Jemma had it when Zach pulled out a worn newspaper clipping of a supposed sighting of the Loch Ness Monster from his wallet. Her eyes got big when he started smoothing out the creases.

"Excuse me," she said as she got her purse and headed toward the bathroom.

In a private section of the same restaurant, Will sat back and smiled at the camaraderie of his co-workers. It was nine people total, and he was glad Mickey wasn't there. Will didn't want to look at his face while he ate. He was anxious to leave because he had gotten Jemma's number from the white pages and wanted to call her. A woman in a white dress walked past their table, and he looked at her. From where he was sitting, Will couldn't see her face, but there was something familiar about the way she walked and the shape of her booty. She stepped to the side to let people pass her in the hallway, and he was startled to see it was Jemma. Will excused himself and headed in that direction. Jemma turned off the water and looked at her reflection in the mirror as she pressed a cold paper towel to her cheeks. She didn't have to use the facilities, but she was stalling so she didn't have to go back to her date. She missed Will so much and wanted to see him. Jemma decided to end the date with Zach. There was no hope for any progression, and she didn't want him to get the wrong idea from their date. She planned on giving Gary an earful about how bad his hook-up was, especially since he had described Zach as the best thing walking on two legs.

"You look yummy in those red heels."

She looked toward the door and thought her eyes were playing tricks on her when she saw Will coming toward her.

"Will?" His name came out in a sound between a gasp and exhale. He had on a charcoal pinstripe suit with a white shirt and tie.

"Wha-what are you doing here? How is this possible?"

He grabbed her hand and led her to the last empty stall. Luckily, there was no one else in the room, and the stall doors were tall and swept the floor. After sliding the lock, he pulled Jemma to him and impatiently kissed her. His tongue entered her mouth, and her fingers cupped his cheeks. *I can kiss her all day*, Will thought as he took a step back and used one hand to brace against the wall as she leaned toward his frame. He eased up on the embrace and tugged on her bottom lip with his teeth before standing to his full height.

"You look beautiful," he said, eyeing her up and down.

"Thanks," she whispered against his lips, and she stared into his dark eyes.

"What are you doing here?"

"I'm having dinner with some people from work." Jemma scowled at his statement.

"Work? But how? You don't live here."

He gave her the short version of how he came to relocate to Chicago, and she was very delighted by the news. "So, you live here now?" she asked, needing to get validation again.

"Yes. I have a house in Country Club Hills."

"Why didn't you tell me in Atlanta?"

"There was a lot going on with the wedding, and there were other things we needed to talk about. What are you doing here?" Jemma bit her lower lip before answering, and his eyebrows went up.

"I promised my co-worker I'd go on a blind date before I left for the wedding. I was just about to cut it short," she replied, and he smirked.

"Yeah, you do that. I'm the only one who's going to take you out." She grinned at that, purring when he started to nuzzle her neck, sniffing her skin. "God, you smell good!" he proclaimed, shoving her dress up.

"Will—"

She gasped as he leaned in to kiss her again, his tender hands running over her behind, fingering her lace thong. Her hands were on his forearms, squeezing as she motioned for the kiss to continue. With one hand, he reached for his trousers, and she moved it away and quickly undid his belt and zipper.

"Be quiet, OK?" he told her in a panting, throaty voice shoving her around so her back was to him.

Jemma didn't know why, but it excited and turned her on when Will roughly bent her over, shoved the underwear to the side, and heaved himself inside her. He palmed her hips and started a fierce pumping action after he settled between her legs.

It was good luck on their part that no one walked into the restroom, especially when feminine grunts escaped from her. The sounds of being repeatedly impaled by him over and over aroused her even more, causing Jemma to have an awesome orgasm. Will kept going until his seed erupted from him and he wrapped one arm around her middle while they tried to catch their breaths.

"That was great."

"Hell, that was more than great," he replied in her ear, and she shivered when his breath reached her spot.

He began to fix his pants and had a lopsided grin as he watched Jemma wiggle her dress down. He motioned her to come to him, and she stepped closer where he took her lips again. They both paused when the door opened and closed, hearing someone hum as the water was turned on and off. Jemma giggled when the lady left, her breath catching when she saw how Will was looking at her.

"Why are you watching me like that?"

"Because I'm happy to see you." She grinned and kissed him on his cheek.

"You better get back to your dinner."

"You're right. I'll call you later."

She nodded, and they carefully left the ladies room. Jemma made an excuse to leave her date and left the eatery. It took her twenty minutes to get home with the traffic on Lake Shore Drive. Once she was safely inside, she took a quick shower and changed into a pair of cotton pajamas. She made a sandwich since she hadn't eaten anything on the disastrous date. An hour and a half later, she got a call from a number she didn't recognize and answered it.

"Hello?"

"Hey, sexy lady," Will said, and she smiled.

∼

WILL WAITED as the iron gates slowly opened and he drove his car up the curved shaped driveway. Michael Vy lived in a gated community in Plainfield, and Will admitted the house looked nice from the outside. After meeting with him at the jail, the arraignment was held a few days later. Because Michael had never been arrested before and didn't have a passport, he wasn't deemed a flight risk, and he was able to go home after his parents paid the expensive bond. Of course, when Michael got home, it was a media circus outside his house, and he did what his lawyer advised; he didn't speak to anyone from the press. Will had given Michael one day to get home and get settled. His parents had moved in with Michael temporarily to help him out and give him emotional support. Will rang the doorbell, and it was answered by Mrs. Vy who had bags under her eyes but still showed spirit in them.

"Hello, Mr. Rutherford," she said, letting him in.

"Good morning, Mrs. Vy. How are you?"

"I'm hanging in there. Michael is waiting for you in the living room." Will followed her, looking around the huge house with expensive trinkets lying about.

Michael was sitting on a long ivory couch, reading what the newspapers were saying about him. He was only twenty years old and still had baby-face features. He was a redbone, had a low-cut hairdo, and was tall for his age.

"Hey, Michael."

"Hi, Mr. Rutherford, what's up?"

"Nothing much. How are you?"

"Going crazy. I can't go outside, my so-called friends won't talk to me, and my former teammates won't take my calls."

Will sat down, looking at his young client. He could tell this was taking a toll on him, and Will went into lawyer mode.

"Naturally, people are going to be wary due to the circumstances, but once you're proven innocent, you can start your life over."

"Do you think the jury will find me innocent?"

"Did you kill your girlfriend?"

"No, I did not."

"Since this will more than likely go to trial, they will find you innocent after I defend you. You said you didn't do it, and I believe you. The only thing I ask is that you do not lie to me. In a case like this, surprises are the last thing we need. Understand?" Michael looked at Will and could see in his eyes that Will believed his innocence.

"Yes, sir." Michael's mother sat next to her son and patted his back.

"I have a good feeling about you, Mr. Rutherford. I looked you up on the web, and you've won a lot of important cases," Mrs. Vy mentioned, observing her son who was still looking defeated.

"I've lost some too, but I will put in solid efforts as your son's lawyer." He opened his briefcase and took out a tape recorder and notepad.

"OK, let's get started. I know when I came to see you in lockup, our time was limited, but we're going to start from the beginning. Give me a history of your relationship with Diana Lake."

Michael waited until his mother left the room, and he did what Will said, watching his lawyer write down key issues.

"Now, tell me about the events leading up until when you found the body." Michael let out a deep breath, taking a sip of his cola.

"Things were strained between us."

"How?"

"We argued a lot. We went for days without talking."

"Why?"

"I don't know. It was like she woke up one day and was a different person. I had a feeling she wanted to tell me something, but she never did. I hadn't heard from her, and after a few days, I went to her apartment."

Will looked up when Michael paused, seeing the distraught look on his face as he prepared to tell the next part.

"I used my key to open the door, walked in, and saw her face down in the living room. I rolled her over, and there was an open gash on her forehead. I tried to get her up and screamed for her to wake up. I started shaking her and crying. I guess the neighbor heard me 'cause the next thing I knew, the cops were there."

"I'll follow up as to who made the call to the police. You said you used your key, so the door was locked?"

"Yes." Will nodded and wrote on his legal pad.

"Does that matter?" Mr. Vy asked, walking in with his wife. It was clear that they had been listening, but Will didn't mind. He was a portly man with a thick beard.

"It does raise some questions like why would your son allegedly kill his girlfriend then lock the door behind himself? Why would he remain at the murder scene? Usually, people flee the scene of a crime, not kill a person and calmly lock the door behind themselves," Will answered, hearing commotion at the front door.

A few seconds later, Will saw a tall female walk toward the kitchen with grocery bags. Michael introduced her to Will as his cousin Tilda.

"No, Tilda can stay. She knew Diana too," Michael told Will after asking his client if he wanted her to stay or go. Will looked at the cousin and something he couldn't name buzzed off inside him.

"How did you know the victim?" Will asked her as she sat down in a chair, a scarf wrapped around her throat. Her hands were interlocked on her lap, and she had long, twisted braids.

"We went to the same school."

"Did she ever confide in you about her relationship with Michael?" Tilda shrugged.

"It was the usual girl talk. They both vented to me about the ups and downs."

"Did you talk to her prior to her death?"

"No," she responded quickly... a little too quickly for Will's taste. He passed a sheet of paper and a pen to Michael. "Write down a list of people who can attest to your relationship... anyone who saw you two together, who saw you fight, etcetera."

"So, what's the next step, Mr. Rutherford?" Mr. Vy asked Will, standing next to the cottage style satin chair where his wife was sitting.

"The preliminary hearing is in two weeks, and yes, you need to be there Michael. At that time, the state prosecutor will present the case and offer probable cause to take Michael to court. My plan is to go to the police station and talk to the arresting officers and get a copy of the report. I'm also going to talk to Diana's neighbors and all the people on Michael's list. I plan to get a second opinion on the autopsy after it's been completed."

"But she died from a blow to the head," Mr. Vy stated with a frown on his face.

"That's the tale, but I want to know what caused that blow. A murder weapon hasn't been found yet. The state will use every way to get the jury to believe that maybe it was a crime of passion, a fight gone wrong, and etcetera. That's why I'm formulating a plan to make visits, calls, and get the paperwork I need," Will reassured them.

"It's good to see that five-thousand-dollar retainer will be put to good use," Mr. Vy mentioned under his breath, and his wife gave him a sly look.

"Mr. Rutherford, is all that necessary?" Tilda asked quietly.

"Yes, it is necessary if you don't want your cousin to go to prison for a crime he didn't commit. I am very precise with my job," Will replied, surprised by her question. What family member wouldn't want their lawyer to do everything to fight for their loved one?

"Mr. Rutherford, you do what you have to do. Michael is our only child. We loved Diana, and we know he didn't kill her," Mr. Vy declared, and Will liked the fact that he was insanely loyal to his son.

"Now, I want you to prepare yourself. The prosecutor is going to put all your business out there and will try to paint you into someone you're not. You don't have a record, you're a public figure, you've donated to several good charities, and you've done community service. You're a model citizen, and that will play in your favor, but all that won't matter when they try to pin a murder rap on you," Will said that last part looking at the entire Vy family. He didn't lie when he said he was going to give it his all, but he wanted to let them know that the next few weeks were going to be rough.

∼

THE NEXT DAY WAS SUNDAY. Will was in his office going over the Vy file. He'd already made plans to go to the police station tomorrow to speak to the arresting officer and the lead detective on the case. Will had a portable whiteboard in his office where he had written down the people from Michael's list. Tilda's name was written on it, and he decided to have another talk with her. He thought he was the only one in the office until Dante walked past his open door.

"Hey. What are you doing here?"

"Good afternoon. I'm just going over the notes for the case."

"Anything interesting?" Dante asked, walking further into the room.

"Michael said he used his key to get into his girlfriend's apartment and that the door was locked."

"That is interesting. He wouldn't take the time to lock the door after committing murder," Dante mumbled.

"That's what I thought."

"Then again, people do odd things after performing a crime."

"That's true too."

"What's your next step?"

"At the arraignment, the judge said the trial would start in sixty days, so I'm going to the police station tomorrow, then will talk to some of the people from his list later in the week," Will answered, and Dante concurred.

"Sounds like you have everything worked out."

"Yeah. What are you doing here on a Sunday, Mr. Fry?"

"I forgot our tickets to the theater tonight. Bonnie threatened to withhold her wifely duties if I didn't come get them," Dante responded, and Will smiled.

"What does your wife do?"

"Bonnie is a retired court clerk. We've been married for twenty-three years."

"That is a blessing, sir."

"Oh, I know. I thank my lucky stars every day she's still with me. Let me ask you a question, son. John told me you were one of the brightest law students he had encountered in a while. What motivates you to do this?" Will knew Dante was referring to Professor Sachs, and Will liked the fact that a senior partner was taking an interest in his career choice. The younger man had a feeling that he did this with all new junior associates.

"There are personal reasons behind it, but I want to be one of the guys who helps put the bad people away and keeps the innocent ones out of jail. I know I won't be able to do it by myself, but knowing there are firms like this one and my previous employer working for the little guy, it helps me feel better about my decision to become a lawyer," Will replied to Dante's question honestly, and the older man nodded.

"That's a good response. It's the weekend, Will. Get out of here. Go catch a movie or something. All of this will be here tomorrow."

"You're right. I just wanted to review what I had."

They conversed for a few more minutes, and Dante left. Will turned toward the desktop and pulled up directions on his computer.

At home, Jemma looked out the open window at the dark clouds and thundering skies. She had the perfect view of Lake Michigan and Navy Pier and could see the fireworks show whenever it happened at the pier. She had the next two days off and was looking forward to relaxing. She turned up the radio, singing to Robert Palmer's "Addicted to Love."

She had on a short-sleeved Smurf shirt with matching high cut blue cotton shorts. Going back to the kitchen, Jemma went to the stove to finish cooking the three cheese tortellini and fried Italian beef sausage. There was half a loaf of Italian bread in the oven with a bottle of wine chilling. She had tried calling Will earlier, but there was no answer at his house. The doorbell rang as she was tasting the red sauce, it was going on 5:30 p.m., and she went to go answer it, not expecting company. She peeked out the peephole, and her heart fluttered when she saw Will on the other side.

"Hi," she greeted him after opening the door.

"Hey."

He walked inside, and when she closed the door, he leaned down to kiss her. She clutched his waist to bring him closer, his hand reaching to stroke her shapely behind. She didn't know what it was about Will's mouth, but it was so enticing and lovely. It seemed like his kisses got better over time and she absolutely adored them.

"It smells good in here," he mentioned against her mouth.

"I'm making dinner."

"Expecting someone?"

"No," she said, rolling her eyes beaming up at him.

"You want to stay for dinner?"

"Yes, thank you." Will took off his blue Nikes, and a few minutes later, they were eating at the bench style kitchen table.

"This is a cozy place," he stated, taking a sip of wine.

"Thanks. Were you in the neighborhood?"

"No. I was at the office prior to coming here."

"Everything good?"

"Yep. Just going over my records for the case."

She watched him as he ate, loving the setting of the moment. It had been a while since she had shared a meal with a person of the opposite sex and was able to have a good conversation to go with it. It was funny because Will was thinking the same thing; it was nice having someone to unwind with after work.

"I've been reading updates in the newspaper about your client. Are you nervous about what will happen in the courtroom?"

"No," he answered truthfully.

"You always were a good cook," he said around a mouthful of pasta. She smiled softly and drank her beverage. Jemma soaked up the sauce with her bread as heavy rain began to fall.

"I went to go see my grandmother," Will stated as she sat back in the seat, folding her legs up under her. Jemma didn't say anything as her eyes searched his.

"What happened?"

"She admitted what she did back then."

"Really?" Will nodded. "Did she say anything else?"

"No."

"That's not surprising," Jemma replied in a low voice.

"I want to apologize for what she did, Jemma."

"It's not your fault, Will, and I'm sorry too."

"I know a lot of time has passed, but I do want to rebuild our relationship."

Jemma wanted to shout for joy at what he'd just said. More than anything, she wanted the same thing, especially since her feelings for him hadn't gone away. She reached across the table and took his hand.

"I want the same thing, Will. Do you think it's possible after all this time?" He glanced at their joined hands before studying her, giving his undivided attention.

"Of course, we'll have to get to know each other again, but I'm willing to put in the work, Jemma. We'll go out, date, talk, and I'm getting you in the bed as often as possible," he answered truthfully, and she chuckled.

"I'm on board with that."

"Good, and we don't let anyone come between us again."

"Also, if we have any issues with one another, we talk it out and work through it," Jemma added, and he agreed. She grinned, feeling the heavy feeling in her stomach dissipate.

"Do you want some more food?" she asked, perusing his bare dinner plate.

"No, I'm fine, babe. Do you work tomorrow?"

"Not until Tuesday."

"Do you have a set schedule at the hospital?"

"No, not really. I usually work five on and two off, but I pick up extra shifts sometimes since I cover two floors."

"You know you stay busy. Don't overwork yourself."

"I'm fine. I'm used to it by now." Will helped her clean the kitchen and load the dishwasher.

They went to go sit on the couch. Jemma carried her wine glass with her. She had a gray couch with the windows to the back of the furniture. There was sand colored carpet throughout the apartment. In the living room, there was an oak bookcase, a twenty-seven-inch big back TV on a stand on the wall opposite from the couch. To the left, was an abstract painting by Pearlie Taylor and a few house plants. A two-tier glass living room table sat a few inches in front of the couch, and Will liked what he saw. From what Jemma had told him, her spare room was an office, there was an extra bathroom, and the master bed and bathroom were in the rear of the apartment.

"How are things going at the law firm? You like your co-workers?"

"So far things are good. I have a great view from my office, although it's not as awesome as yours. My co-workers are cool." He didn't tell her about Mickey because he didn't want to waste time talking about the douchebag.

Jemma had folded her legs Indian style and was facing Will. He had his arm stretched across the back of the couch and his feet crossed at the ankles. It was gloomy outside due to the rain clouds, but she didn't turn on the lamp. She felt comfortable sitting in the semi-dark room with him, and a rapid succession of lightning bolts flashed across the grayish sky. She licked her lips after taking a sip of wine, and Will felt a tugging at his groin. *She is so fucking sexy!*

"Are you in a rush to get home?" The rain had Jemma feeling some type of way. That and the fact that Will was sitting next to her, looking and smelling terrific.

"No, why do you ask?" She didn't say anything as she crawled over to him and undid his jeans, her hard nipples pressing against the Smurf shirt distracting him. Will let out a low, rumbling sigh when Jemma tugged down his pants and lowered her head to his thumping penis.

CHAPTER 3

Jemma ran a hand over the back of her neck, trying to ease the knot. She had been upstairs on the labor and delivery floor since seven in the morning, and it had been non-stop baby insanity. It seemed like every woman that came in was ready to bring a new life into the world. So far, she had assisted on three births and the last one ended up being difficult because the baby was born ten pounds and the mother had to get stitches. She finished entering the post-delivery notes into the computer for the new mommies, and she grabbed her can of ginger ale.

"Is all this making you get baby fever?" Another nurse named Anne asked Jemma, and she shook her head.

"No, not right now. It's making me want a bowl of potato soup, though." Anne laughed, popping a piece of candy into her mouth. Anne was a short, Asian nurse with long, jet-black hair.

"Who eats soup in the summertime?"

"I know. I'm weird," Jemma had on mint green scrubs with baby animals on them. "Let's go to lunch after we make our rounds," Anne suggested, and Jemma nodded. They left from behind the registration desk, and they parted ways as they headed toward the east and west wings of the floor. Jemma walked into one room where a woman was looking at daytime TV.

"Hello, Mrs. Griffin. How are you feeling?" Jemma asked, picking up her chart and heading toward the fetal monitor.

"I'm doing well... a few contractions here and there," the petite woman replied, rubbing her belly.

"Yes, I see." Jemma looked at the paper graph that was slowly running out the monitor and made some notes on her chart. "Everything is looking good on the screen. Baby's heartbeat is good and strong. Has the doctor been in yet?"

"Not since earlier."

"Well, it's been a shift change, but he should be here shortly. Do you need anything?"

"Some ice chips would be great," Mrs. Griffin answered with a rueful grin.

"Not a problem. Where's your husband?"

"He went to the cafeteria; he said he was starving."

"I can have food service bring an extra tray for him, so he won't have to leave and possibly miss something."

"Oh, that'll be great. Thank you."

Jemma nodded with a smile and went to the whiteout board to update it. She wrote her name as the nurse on call and Dr. Oivan as the physician on duty.

"I'll be right back with the ice," Jemma said, leaving the room.

"Hey, Jemma, Ms. Ruben is asking for some slippers. Can you take her a pair?" A CNA named Gina asked, passing her in the hall, and Jemma nodded.

"Yep, she's the next patient I'm seeing."

When she got back to Mrs. Griffin's room, her husband was there, and they were smiling at each other.

"Here you go," she said placing the cup on the table next to the bed. "Do you need anything else?"

"No, I'm fine. Thanks."

"Okay. If you need me, just push the call button. You get some rest. It's going to be a while since you're only three centimeters dilated," Jemma informed the patient, patting her on the shoulder.

"Will you be here for a while?" Mrs. Griffin asked just as Jemma reached the door.

"Yes. I'm on until midnight, and hopefully, I'll get to meet your first born by then," Jemma replied.

"I hope so too," Mr. Griffin added under his breath and Jemma laughed softly.

Stopping by the supply room, she grabbed a pair of large blue footies and headed to Ms. Ruben's room.

"Hi, Ms. Ruben," Jemma said, holding up the footwear.

"It's about time you got here! My feet are freezing," the brunette said in a snappish tone.

"I'm sorry. I'm making my rounds, and I got to you as soon as I could," Jemma explained, slipping them on her feet.

"Whatever. I'm hungry." Jemma grabbed her chart and checked her vitals.

"Unfortunately, you can't have any food right now," Jemma said distractedly while checking the baby monitor.

"Well, what am I supposed to do? I haven't had anything to eat since yesterday."

"I can maybe get you a popsicle," Jemma said, resting her arms on the bedrail. Ms. Ruben had been a difficult patient since being admitted to the floor. She had a surly attitude with everyone who went into her room and was an overall grouch.

"A popsicle? What am I? Five years old? I want a cheeseburger."

"That's not going to happen right now, Ms. Ruben," Jemma explained calmly, and she looked at the anxious woman, noticing she was there alone.

"Is there someone I can call for you? A family member or friend?" Ms. Ruben looked away from Jemma, ignoring her.

"No, it's just me." Jemma didn't say anything for a minute. "Okay. Well, the doctor should be coming by to see you shortly. Just let me know if you need anything else."

Jemma updated the whiteout board in Ms. Ruben's room so she

could know who to ask for. She stopped by three other rooms and made the moms-to-be as comfortable as possible. She met Anne at the elevators, and they went to the cafeteria together. Jemma usually ate light, but because it was 2:15 p.m., and she was there for at least another ten hours, she grabbed two orders of tuna salad.

∾

WILL WAS at the seventeenth precinct waiting to talk to Detective King. He was the lead detective on the Diana Lake murder case, and he agreed to speak to Will about the investigation. It was a lot going on at the station; phones were ringing, and people were walking around in uniforms and in plain clothes. Criminals in handcuffs were being escorted, and monitors were going on and off.

"Sorry for the wait, Mr. Rutherford. It's a madhouse in here," the cop said as he sat down with a file.

"It's okay. Thanks for seeing me today."

"You're representing Michael Vy?"

"Yes. That's why I'm here to get info about the case."

"You look young to be a lawyer," King said, sitting back to play with his pen, and Will smiled at that.

"I get that a lot."

Detective Grayson King was a thirty-year vet on the job and had seen everything humanly possible crime-wise. He was a tall man with dark skin and salt and pepper hair that was evident in his facial whiskers.

"What can you tell me about the Lake case?"

"Well, I'm sure you know the logistics, but Diana Lake was a twenty-three-year-old African-American female who died of apparent blunt force trauma to the head. Officers arrived at the scene and saw your client covered in the victim's blood and very upset. After he was put in the squad car, the neighbor who called 911 told them that she had heard arguing a week prior to her death and heard more arguing the same day Ms. Lake died," the cop said, reading from the report.

"What prompted her to call the police?" Will was quiet as he watched Detective King read over the file.

"It says here she heard a scuffle."

"Okay. Can I get a copy of that and of the crime scene photos?"

"Not a problem, counselor."

"What is being done to catch Ms. Lake's real killer? You don't have a confession, no murder weapon, and no evidence against my client," Will declared, and Grayson glared at Will while slowly springing backward and forward in the worn, wooden chair.

"We're still investigating. The medical examiner is still working on the body, but the arguing and bruises on the victim's body tell a different story."

"And that is going to tell the jury that Mr. Vy killed Ms. Lake in a lover's quarrel?"

Will looked up as Lori Santiago walked up to Detective King's desk with a briefcase in her hand. She was the Puerto Rican state's assistant district attorney that was prosecuting the Vy case. They had initially met at the preliminary hearing, and Lori had offered a deal for Michael, but Will declined it.

"Miss. Santiago, how nice to see you."

"Mr. Rutherford, fancy meeting you here." She was as tall as Will and had on a black dress with a blue professional jacket over it with her light brown hair hanging down her back.

"Just doing my job. You mind telling me what that last sentence was about?"

"I just came from the medical examiner's office. The cause of death has been officially determined, and the bruises on her arms match your client's fingerprints," Lori said with a smirk that didn't bother Will.

"You do know that he did grab her when he discovered the body? He was distressed at finding his dead girlfriend's body." Will was standing up with his hands in his pocket, needing to be eye-to-eye when he spoke to the ADA.

"Whatever you say. You might want to go to the coroner's office.

Her findings just put the icing on the cake for my case. Your client is going away for a long time."

The detective came back with the copies for Will, and he hailed a cab to go to the medical examiner's building. Lori Santiago had a smug look on her face that he didn't like.

∽

Mr. Vy rushed to the door as Will repeatedly pressed the doorbell. He had just left the coroner's office, and he was beyond pissed!

"Mr. Rutherford! What—"

"Where is Michael?"

"In the kitchen with his mother." He headed in the correct direction, his shoes echoing on the hardwood floors.

"Hi, Mr.—"

"What did I say? What was the first thing I said to you, Michael?" Will interrupted Mrs. Vy's greeting as his father followed Will into the kitchen. It looked as though he had disturbed their lunch because it was a pizza box on the table.

"Mr. Rutherford, I—"

"Answer the question!" Will barked.

"Not to lie to you... to tell everything up front."

"And why didn't you? You have to be straight up with me if we're going to prove you're innocent."

"What the hell are you talking about?" Mr. Vy questioned as he stood between his wife and son.

"I'm talking about the fact that Diana Lake was nine weeks pregnant," Will delivered the news and watched as genuine shock crossed over the faces of the Vy family.

"P-pregnant?" Michael panted out, looking at Will, and his lawyer nodded.

Mr. and Mrs. Vy looked at each other, tears falling down the eyes of the latter. Will stood in the quiet room, waiting for someone to say something.

"I-I didn't know, Will. I swear to God. Diana didn't tell me. Dad, I didn't know." Mr. Vy nodded and went toward his son and gave him a tight hug.

Will watched everyone and had a sense that they weren't aware of the pregnancy. "You really didn't know, Michael?"

"I swear to you; I didn't know. Nine weeks? Jesus, why didn't she tell me?" Michael asked himself more than anyone, holding his head in his hands.

"They found bruises on her arms that match your prints. The ADA is going to use that and say you two were arguing, you grabbed her, things got out of hand, and you pushed her," Will explained to his client, who looked like he was about to throw up.

"But I didn't! I did grab her, but it was after I found her body." Will nodded and let out a strained breath. "OK. You have to be at the medical examiner's office on Thursday so they can do a DNA test for you," Will told him, and he seemed shocked.

"But why? They were in an exclusive relationship," Mrs. Vy asked, wiping her tears away. "I just want to make sure. This information is a damn game changer."

The husband and wife looked at each other despairingly after what he'd just said.

～

JEMMA WAS in the employee lounge at her locker when Gary walked in. "You still not gonna tell me who sent you those flowers?" Jemma looked over at the round table where a vase of two dozen red and white roses mixed together. They were in full bloom and so pretty.

"Nope."

"Heffa."

She grinned and pulled out her umbrella. It was turning out to be the wettest summer so far, and Jemma didn't mind. "You heading home?"

"Yes. I'm taking a nice, long shower and going to bed. When do you get off?"

"At ten."

"OK, I'll call you later."

Because of the rain and the traffic, it was exactly 4:30 p.m. when she got home. She had been at work since sunrise and was exhausted. She was glad when she'd be back on her regular shift after that day; she didn't like the overnight or early morning schedules because it threw off her sleep pattern.

After placing the vase on the kitchen table, she walked into her bedroom, taking off her socks. The bed was calling her name, but she knew if she sat on it, that would be the end. Walking into her connecting bathroom, she pulled back the curtain and turned on the shower. After discarding her work clothes in the hamper, she was about to get in when her phone rang.

"Hello?"

"Hey, Jemma."

"Hi, Will. What's going on?" she asked with a small grin.

"Ugh, tired. Had a bombshell hit my case today."

"Oh no. That sucks."

"Tell me about it, but it'll work itself out. What are you doing?"

"About to hop in the shower and go to bed."

"No, no. Don't do that. Have you eaten yet? I'll come over with food." She chuckled. "You're silly. What are you getting?"

"I don't know yet. I'll stop and get something. Do you work tomorrow?"

"No, I have the weekend off, which is a rarity," she added.

"Good. You can show me the sights of the city."

"Chicago is a big place; you won't be able to see everything in a day, honey."

"I'm sure I won't, but it's supposed to be nice tomorrow, and we can spend the day together."

"I would like that," she replied with a true smile.

"OK, so don't fall asleep on me," he insisted urgently, and she shook her head.

"I won't." She hung up, still pleased and went to go shower before Will showed up.

Afterward, she turned on the TV in the bedroom after applying her scented lotion and putting on a pink jersey sleep shirt. Before she could see what was on the TV, her eyes closed, and she was in a deep slumber. The sound of the doorbell startled her awake, and she rubbed her eyes. It felt like she was napping for only a few seconds, but when she looked at her clock, she saw that two hours had passed.

"You fell asleep, didn't you?" Will asked when she let him in, carrying takeout and an overnight bag.

She smiled softly, her eyes fatigued. "No. I only dozed off."

His clothes were wet from the rain, and he took his shoes off before carrying the food into the kitchen.

"What did you get?"

"Stopped off for Chinese food." He took his gray jacket off, and she hung it up so it could dry. She got out eatery, and soon they were eating the hot food.

"How was your day?" she asked, taking a bite of a veggie eggroll. "The rest of the day was uneventful. I had to take a few aspirins earlier."

"Is everything OK?"

"Yes. What about you?" he returned the question.

"It was fine. I hate working the early morning shift; it throws off my clock."

"Do you work that schedule often?"

"Every month, we have to rotate those different schedules. If you hadn't called, I would've still been sleep and probably up all night."

"Well, I guess it's a good thing I called, huh?" She smirked, taking a sip of her bottled water.

He watched her, and amusement passed across his face. He once again thanked God that she had been made available to him again.

"What's with the look?"

"I was just thanking my luck that you were single and able to be back in my life." She smiled at that as she looked into his eyes.

"I thought about that as well. Most people don't get the opportunity to have a second chance to start over."

He agreed with that, and that's why he wasn't going to take this occasion for granted. He knew there was a lot going on in both of their lives, but he thought things were going well with them. He knew they couldn't pick up where they left off, but they couldn't exactly jump into it either. "You're thinking about something too hard, Will." He looked up at her and saw her scrutinizing him under an intense gaze.

"You're quite perceptive today," he mentioned, and she shrugged.

"Are you thinking about your case?"

"No, it was about us."

"Good or bad thoughts?" Jemma asked softly, staring into his eyes.

"I just want to be sure that us getting back together is what we both want. I don't want you to feel pressured or forced because it's something I want," he told her, and she didn't speak as she looked at him. Jemma shook her head while glaring at him.

"I'm not a violent person, but you're gonna make me slap you. I was miserable without you, Will. I cried myself to sleep so many nights after I left Howard. I don't have any doubts at all that I want to be with you," she responded to what he had said, and inside he felt ecstatic.

"OK, baby. I was just making sure." She made an exasperated face and went back to her fried rice. "By the way, I might like that slap you mentioned." Jemma choked on her food and took a sip of water before roaring with laughter.

~

WILL and Jemma were walking hand-in-hand at Navy Pier. It was a lot of people inside and outside of the place; the crowded attraction showing that people wanted to get out and enjoy the summer weather. They had gotten up early and drove around to see the sites of the city in his green Cadillac Seville. She had shown him Comiskey Park, the United Center, and Soldier Field. He parked his car in a lot on Wabash, and they had taken the bus on Michigan Avenue, getting off at the Wrigley Building to walk down the occupied street. They went shopping at Nordstrom's and the Water Tower Place and had a light lunch. It was 8:15 p.m., and they had stopped along the thick ropes to admire the peaceful water. Will had on a yellow collared shirt with jeans and sneakers, and Jemma was wearing a purple thin striped top with white shorts and matching sandals.

"How do you like what you've seen so far?" Jemma asked as he placed his hands on her hips, their bags on the ground in front of her.

"I love it. This is a charming city; it's a lot going on in the summer," he said, remembering when she told him of all the festivals and events that took place in the warmer months. She leaned up to kiss his cheek, breathing in his warmth at his neck.

"I'm glad you like it," she whispered, her breath tingling his skin.

"Are you ready to go?" She nodded, her hands covering his arms. "I'm looking forward to seeing your home." Jemma was spending the night at his house, and he hoped she liked it.

"Let's head back to the car. It's a long drive from here to the suburbs." They picked up tacos for dinner before heading to Country Club Hills. Forty-five minutes later, they pulled up in his two-car garage, and they entered his house from there. To the right was a small laundry room and through a connecting door was a big kitchen with a marble island. There was a big oak table in the dining room that was across the patio doors. He showed her the unfurnished basement, the downstairs bathroom, the living room with a working fireplace, and upstairs, there were three bedrooms. The main bedroom was huge with a big connecting bathroom that had a big shower. She really liked the tall ceilings and the fact that she could look down to the first floor from the iron banister on the second floor.

"This is beyond wonderful!" Jemma exclaimed after he had given her the tour of his house.

"It could use a woman's touch," he revealed, sitting on the arm of the sofa. She walked over to him and leaned on his lap, draping her left arm around his neck. "So, I should put those little decorative soaps in the bathroom and bowls of potpourri on the dining room table?"

"If you want to, darling. Go nuts." She laughed at that.

"I do want to try out that jacuzzi upstairs tonight," she told him, and he let out a sly grin. "That can be arranged. I can light some candles... play some soft music."

"Hmm... that sounds romantic," she purred against him and kissed his lips. Will took her hand, and they went upstairs, leaving their food on the kitchen counter.

CHAPTER 4

Will held the phone to his ear, waiting for his brother to pick up. He hadn't spoken to Robert since the wedding, and he wanted to check in with him. Usually, when Will called, he had to leave a message because his brother was never home, and Robert would call back at his earliest convenience. But when Robert picked up on the fourth ring, Will was surprised.

"Hello?"

"Hey! I thought I was going to have to leave you a voicemail."

"I had to turn the stove off before I answered. I have a date coming over in an hour."

"Ooh, is this a special lady in your life?" Will had put in ten hours in the office today, and he was relaxing at home with his feet up watching *The Godfather*.

"I'm not sure. We've been trying to have this dinner for months, and now, it's finally happening."

"Tell me you're not making that salty ass jambalaya of yours?" Will asked with a grin, taking a swallow of his beer.

"It's gumbo, you creep, and it's not salty. I've improved my recipe, and whenever you bring your bow-legged ass for a visit, I'll make it for you," Robert retorted, sitting on the bar stool at the kitchen counter. "I'll hold you to that. Just make sure you have plenty of water on deck for my visit."

"Is this the reason for your call? To critique my cooking skills?" Robert asked, playing with the wooden spoon that was sitting in front of him.

"No, I'm just checking in. I haven't talked to you since Atlanta."

"I'm good, bro. How are you? How's your case working out?"

"It's going. Making progress, not making progress."

"You got this, Will. Anything else going on?"

"Well, Jemma and I are back talking. We're having another go at things."

Robert's mouth popped open, and he was shocked and happy to hear the news. "Get out! That's good, Will. So, you guys talked and everything?"

"Yes. I went to go see Grams, and she admitted it." Robert shook his head, not wanting to go down that road regarding his grandmother.

"That's crazy. I'm glad you are trying to make it work with her."

"Me too."

"I like Jemma. She's the only girl I know that can hold her own with you."

"She can get pretty feisty," Will replied with a knowing grin. "What's the name of your dinner date?"

"Elizabeth. She's a cutie, too."

"Well, I hope it's a successful date."

"We'll see."

The brothers talked for another fifteen minutes before disconnecting the call. Will wanted to call Jemma, but he knew that she was at the hospital working a shift.

∼

A WEEK LATER, Will was in his office making notes on his computer for the Vy case. He had spent the last three days in court making jury selections. He was still waiting on the results of the DNA test which according to the medical examiner, weren't at the top of her list since the initial autopsy had been conducted. He had talked to Diana's neighbor and knew he was going to call the woman as a witness for the defense. Will had also spoken to Diana's parents, and they had nothing but good things to say about Michael. He still had to speak to the coach and some of his teammates. That was proving difficult because it was the off season, and they tended to scatter to different locations afterward. However, he'd track down everyone on the list eventually.

"Okay, Mr. Rutherford, I was able to track down Michael's coach. He's at his summer home in Grand Rapids, and I have addresses to the teammates he wrote on his list. Looks like you're going to have to do some driving," Kelly told him as she walked into his office and handed him the paper she'd printed out.

"Grand Rapids? Shit, that's a drive."

"It's not that far; it's maybe three hours," she told him, sitting in the chair with her notebook in her lap. She was wearing a white blouse that was too big and a long skirt that reached her ankles.

"That doesn't sound too bad. Opening arguments are in a few weeks, and I have to get this taken care of tomorrow."

"I'll keep trying to locate the other people on the list while you're gone, Mr. Rutherford."

"Kelly, I told you it's fine if you call me Will." She nodded and looked down at her lap again.

"So, have you been keeping up with the news regarding the case?" Will tried to engage her in conversation because they were co-workers, and she seemed like a nice person. Kelly was the mousiest woman he'd ever met and wondered why she was so shy; it was like she was hesitant to speak up or something.

"Only when I catch the news, yes. If you'll excuse me, I'll go finish working on the list." She left the office before he could say anything, and Will shook his head. Fiona knocked on his door a few minutes later, and Will smiled at his secretary.

"Hey, boss. Do you mind if I leave early today? Some of the other secretaries are going out for drinks, and I want to go home and change," Fiona said happily, walking further into the office. She was wearing a forest green skirt with a matching short jacket.

"Absolutely, Fiona. What am I going to say? No, you stay here and work until midnight?" She grinned at his non-annoyed face and words.

"OK, I just wanted to make sure it was fine."

"Fiona, you've been working hard these last few weeks as well. Go and have some fun." She tilted her head and placed her hands on her hips.

"Didn't I say something like that to you a few weeks ago?"

"You did. I'm just repeating wise words from my awesome secretary. So, how many people are going out for drinks?"

"So far, it's five, but we're waiting to hear from some others."

"OK. Don't overdo it and start drunk dialing people," Will lightly warned her, and she laughed at that. "I saw Kelly leave your office."

"Is she supposed to go out as well?"

"She was invited but declined. She's so shy!"

"I know. It's as if she's scared to talk; like if she says something, it will be dismissed." Will mentioned, and Fiona nodded.

"Usually if people are like that, it has something to do with the way they were raised," Fiona returned as Will replaced the cap on his pen.

"Hopefully, she'll come out her shell. I'm going to leave as well and catch up with Jemma." They both packed up their things and left the office. Will extended his wishes to Fiona that she have a good time.

∽

JEMMA JUMPED and clapped her hand when she knocked down nine pins with her bowling ball. It was Thursday night, and she was out bowling with Phoebe, Gary, and some other people from the hospital. They almost never had the same night off, and they'd wanted to take advantage of it. She had called Will's office to invite him and left a message with Fiona, but she didn't know if he had received it or not. She was wearing blue jean shorts and a cranberry colored tank top.

"Good job, Jemma."

"Thanks, Evan," she responded to Dr. Langham. Altogether, there were eleven people; some were bowling, and the rest were just sitting around, drinking and talking. For it to be a weekday, it was packed at Cosmo's Bowling Hole which was located in the downtown area near the Chicago River. In addition to the bowling lanes, it had a bar, restaurant and pool tables.

"You know, honey, I'm not going to get beaten by you tonight," Gary said, wrapping an arm around Jemma's neck, and she smiled.

"That's a hard thing to say when you're down by eighteen pins."

"I'm going to make my move. Don't worry."

"Give it up, sugar. You're the worst bowler ever," his boyfriend, Tony said, and Phoebe tittered. Her husband, Logan, had walked up at the last part from coming back from the restroom.

"Who's the worst bowler?"

"Gary," Phoebe replied, sitting on his lap.

"I'm making a comeback," he mumbled.

"I'm going to go place an order for more party wings," Jemma announced, and Evan stood up too.

"I'll come with you."

They walked to the restaurant and waited at the register while the people in front of them were being serviced. "Are you having fun?" Evan asked, and she nodded. "Yes, I like when we all can go out and kick it."

"It is a nice break from the hospital." She nodded again and looked around the full establishment. Evan thought this was the perfect time to make his move since they were away from listening ears.

"Hey, Jemma, I was wondering if we could go out; just the two of us?" She looked at him, feeling bad that she would have to turn him down, especially since he was such a nice guy.

"Evan, that was nice of you to ask. You're such a sweetheart, but I'm seeing someone, and I'm crazy about him. It wouldn't be fair to you." He let out a heavy breath and nodded.

"Can't blame a guy for trying. But if he does screw up what he has with you, I'll be there."

"I'm not going to screw anything up. She's mine!" a baritone voice snarled from behind them, and they turned to see Will standing there. He had his suit jacket off, and the tie had been loosened. Jemma smiled and introduced the two guys.

"Nice to meet you, doc."

"Same here. Excuse me." Evan left them alone, and Will looked at Jemma, who grinned again.

"Hi. I'm glad you showed up." Will tugged on her hand and cupped her cheek to kiss her. She returned the smooch slowly, not caring about the looks they were getting.

"I didn't know if you had gotten my message or not."

"I did. How long have you been here?"

"About two hours. C'mon. I want you to meet my friends."

Walking with joined hands, they went over to the group, and she introduced Will. Jemma grinning when Phoebe and Greg mouthed *Wow*.

"You bowling with us, Will?" Logan asked as a new game was starting.

"No, I'll just watch. Thanks."

"How was your day?" Jemma asked, opting out the next game. "It was fine. It's nice to see you out having fun."

"You should be having fun too."

"I'm good."

"Have you had anything to eat?"

"Earlier." They looked up as the crowd yelled in excitement when Tony bowled a strike. "What's wrong, honey? I'm getting a feeling from you."

"I'm just exhausted."

"You didn't have to come out if you're tired," she said to him, covering his hand with hers. They both looked toward the pool area when a fight broke out.

"Damnit! Can't enjoy one night out," Logan spoke, pulling out his badge and heading toward the ruckus.

"Let's go," Will said to Jemma and waited as she grabbed her purse and said goodbye to Gary and Phoebe. They left the bowling alley and walked toward her parked car.

Will pressed Jemma against the Jeep and began to kiss her. She wrapped her arms around his neck, continuing the kiss. When it was over, he told her about his plan to drive out of town tomorrow. She knew she couldn't go with him and wished he didn't have to drive by himself.

"What time are you heading out to Grand Rapids?"

"At seven. The coach knows I'm coming, and the sooner I get there, the sooner I get back and can go see the other people."

"Please be careful driving."

"I will, sweetheart. I'll input the directions into my GPS, and I have roadside assistance in case something happens."

"OK, good. What time do you think you'll be back?"

"It'll be late, but I'll call you, so you don't worry."

"Oh, you know me so well," she said dryly.

"I should hope so. Do you work on Saturday?" Will asked as he curled his fingers around her derrière.

"No."

"You should come to the house. I'll make lunch."

"You're going to cook? Oh, this I have to see," Jemma said with a giggle.

"Stop being a smartass," he replied, pulling her closer to him.

∼

WILL WAS IN HIS GARAGE, washing his car two days later. He had on a pair of jeans with no shirt, and they were low-slung on his hips. The radio that was sitting on the workbench was on WGCI, and The Commodores were playing. He had just washed the soap off his car and was wiping it down with a terry cloth. Shadowy clouds had been forming all day, and they had just opened to release a light rainfall. He was keeping the beef penne pasta with crushed red peppers warm on the stove for Jemma. The cordless phone rang, and he threw down the damp towel before picking up the device.

"Hello?"

"Hey Will," Joshua said from the other end, his voice still blooming and clear.

"Hey, grandad. How are you?"

"I'm fine and dandy. I just got off the phone with your brother and now I'm calling you to see how you're doing. How are things going at the law firm?"

"It's going good so far, been getting things ready for court in a few weeks."

"I've seen the news reports about the case. It's made national news. I even saved some clippings from newspaper's. Will grinned at that; Joshua has always been one of his biggest supporters.

"Yeah, the media has been crazy here."

"I bet. So, anything else going on with you? The question had an open-ended feel to it and Will had a feeling Robert mentioned Jemma to their grandfather.

"Well, I'm not sure if you already know, but I'm back with Jemma."

"I heard," Joshua replied with a hearty grin. *Robert and his damn big mouth,* Will silently cursed. "I'm glad to hear that. I always liked Jemma. How have she been?"

"She moved back to Chicago after graduating and has been a nurse for a few years."

"Now, that's all right. Robert told me about Mona's role into your breakup; can't say I wasn't surprised." Joshua knew first hand how Mona could be and sadly that was normal behavior for her.

"I don't even want to talk about it, granddad. We're back together and we're making things work."

"I am glad to hear that. I saw the light in your eyes and Jemma's eyes and I know she made you happy." Will didn't know that Joshua could see how external their feelings had been in college, but he was glad.

"How is Thelma doing?" Will knew she had been a fixture in Joshua's life since his divorce from Mona and he liked her when they met years ago. Will could hear the vibe in his grandfather's voice change to pleasantness and that answered his question.

"She's is all right. We're actually flying out to California at the end of the week. She said she wants to go see Hollywood and take one of those movie studio tours, so we're going to be there for ten days," Joshua replied, and Will nodded with approval.

"Oh, she'll love that.

"Yeah, it'll be nice to get away from things for a while."

"Is everything ok at the company?" Will asked with concern.

"Yes, everything is good. It'll just be nice to get away from paperwork, meetings and boardrooms.

"If anyone deserves a vacation, it's you."

"You sound like Thelma," Joshua answered with a chuckle. "Well, I don't won't keep you. Thelma is on the way over and we're going to an art gallery opening.

"That's sounds fun, granddad."

"Yeah, it's a big thing and we got tickets because Thelma is a friend of the mother of one of the painters." After talking for a few more minutes, they exchanged farewells and Will hung up the phone. That put him in good spirits; knowing Joshua was out having fun and being active with Thelma. Will looked up as Jemma pulled into the open garage. The top was down on her Jeep, and she had been dusted with some rain. The car radio played Elton John's "Rocket Man."

Will was looking so delicious and manly with no shirt on and his muscles solid and flexing. Jemma slowly licked her lips, the unmistakable look of lust and wanting visible in her eyes. She watched as he threw the damp towel on the hood of the Cadillac and walked over to her car. After climbing in, he pushed the passenger seat back to accommodate his height. She undid the seatbelt, and she sat astride on his lap without waiting for permission. His hands pushed up her blue jean dress. She clasped his neck and released a shaky huff before bending her head to kiss him at an unhurried pace. Jemma was turned on by the fact that they were in the garage where anyone could see them. The only light came from the open door.

Will was fumbling with his pants between their bodies, and she released a content breath when he lifted and impaled her on him. She placed her hands on his shoulders and started to move up and down; Will grabbing her ass to keep the motion going. Her breasts became sensitive and full against her bra. Her nipples pushed against cloth. Will quickly undid the top buttons to her dress and lifted her right breast as he was ravenously sucking on her nipple. She liked hearing his grunts, and she tossed her head back when she increased her movements. After their heated orgasms, she kissed him again and gently nipped at his bottom lip.

"I cooked," Will mentioned, rubbing his thumbs over her distended, visible areolas.

"I know. I'm very excited about that," she said in a breathless tone.

"I bet you are," he retorted, giving her tush a hard slap. She made an animated sound, and he inwardly grinned. "Come on and let me feed you."

They left the garage, and he placed her small night bag by the couch. They ate the food, and Will took a sip of wine watching Jemma eat the pasta.

"This is yummy, Will,"

"Glad you like it. You know since we've been back together, we haven't said we love one another." She looked at him and placed her chin in her hand.

"You're right, Will. I still feel like I'm walking on eggshells. I don't want things to get screwed up again," she let him know, and he nodded.

"I can understand that. Do you still love me, Jemma?"

"Yes," she stated without faltering.

"Say it."

"I love you, William Edward Rutherford."

"Dang, used my whole government name…" he mumbled under his breath, causing her to chortle. "I love you, Jemma Alden. I would use your middle name, but you don't have one. I love the girl I met in college, and I'm looking forward to loving the woman that you've turned into," Will said, reaching out to hold her hand.

"That's lovely, Will. You've grown into a man I already love."

"You're such a sweet talker."

"I'm just being honest."

"I know, love." She kissed the back of his hand, and they finished their meal. Because the weather was crappy, they didn't mind staying in the house. Will got a fire going, and they ended up playing several games of Uno.

~

Two weeks later, Will was working on his opening statement, which was scheduled for next week. The month had passed by quickly, and they would be in the courtroom before he knew it. The closer the date got, the crazier the press became. They hounded the Vy and Lake families by trying to get a statement or a slip up on Michael's part, and Will was glad he was following his directive and didn't speak to the media. He had spent time going over prep questions with Michael and tutored him on how to answer questions from the ADA. Will had called for the paternity results again and was told it was in process... the same answer he'd gotten since the test was initially performed.

Michael's cousin, Tilda, had come in a few days ago since Will had called her in to ask her a few more questions. She was uneasy being around Will, and he had put her mind at ease, even though there was something about her that was off. The intercom buzzed, and he looked up in annoyance.

"Fiona, I said no calls!" Will snapped, looking at his legal pad.

"It's Jemma, but I'll tell her you're unavailable."

"No, you can put her through." He picked up the phone glad to hear her voice.

"Hey, babe," she said, closing the oven door after checking the food.

"Hi," he replied with a sigh.

"You sound exhausted."

"No, I'm good. What's going on?" "Nothing. Just cooking. Have you had lunch?"

"I had coffee and a bagel this morning."

"It's after 1:30 p.m., you need to eat, Will."

"I'll send out for something," Will relented with a sigh.

"OK, well, I won't keep you. I just wanted to say hi. Can you put me back on with Mrs. Lopez?"

"Why?" "I want to tell her to have a good day." He transferred the call back to Fiona, who answered on the first ring.

"Is Will OK?"

"Not really. He gets like this when it's close to trial. He doesn't eat much, and he's running around like a freight train."

"Is he being a grouch?"

"Yes and no. He knows not to be one with me. I'll tap his knuckles extra hard with a ruler." Jemma smiled and went to her closet to find something to wear.

"I'll bring him some food. Don't let him order anything."

Fiona scoffed at the idea. "Don't worry. He'll be too busy to call for takeout."

∼

JEMMA LOOKED at the glowing lights in the elevator as it made its way to the eighteenth floor. She was holding a wicker basket with both hands; the aroma of the hot food filled the compartment. She had on a peach and white sundress with spaghetti straps that flared out and peach strappy flip-flops. The elevator doors opened, and she walked toward Will's office per Fiona's directions. She liked how the floor was decorated with the matching carpet to the two-tone walls. It was 4:45 p.m., and she didn't see the legal secretary sitting at her desk. In fact, it had been cleaned off, and the computer had been shut down.

The office door was open, and when she peeked in, she saw Will on the phone with his back toward her, and there was a girl sitting on the couch, writing something on a legal pad. Jemma knocked on the door, and they both turned toward the sound. He released a big smile and held up his index finger while he finished his call.

"Can I help you?" Kelly asked, standing up.

"I'm here to see Will."

"He should be done with his call shortly. Would you like something to drink?" Kelly asked Jemma quietly, and she shook her head.

"No, thank you."

Will hung up the phone and turned toward the two women. "We're done for the day, Kelly. You can go home." Kelly nodded and left the office, and Will closed the door and locked it.

"Who was that?" Jemma asked, placing the basket on the glass table and tossing her purse on the couch.

"A paralegal who's been assigned to help with the case."

"She seems nice," Jemma mumbled as he walked toward her.

"What are you doing here, honey?"

"I bought you a late lunch or an early dinner, depending on what you want to call it." As soon as she said that, Jemma heard his stomach growl. "I take it you didn't get any food."

"I didn't. Time got away from me," he replied, and she rolled her eyes.

"Well, luckily for you, I have some goodies I think you'll like."

"It does smell delicious. What do you have?" he asked, peeking over her shoulder.

Jemma went over to the basket to take out containers, and Will cocked his head to get a glimpse of her upper thighs under her dress.

"I have cornbread, pot roast with carrots, and potatoes."

"Well damn, girl! What made you cook all this?"

She sat down on the couch and pulled out plastic cutlery as he turned one of the hard-back chairs to face her. "I cooked it to take to lunch for work, but I thought you'd like to share with me as well."

Will was wearing tan trousers with a light blue shirt, and his tie had been removed since it was after hours. "Thank you for bringing me nourishment."

"You're welcome, baby. This is a nice office, Will."

"Thanks. It's bigger than my last one." He ate a piece of the tender meat and closed his eyes. "I swear, you should open up your own restaurant." Her mouth curved upward, eating some potatoes. "You're going to make me soft in the middle with all your good cooking."

"That's fine. It's just more for me to squeeze."

Will didn't think he couldn't love Jemma anymore after her words. He took them as she would love him if his body type changed or not.

They finished eating while continuing their talk, and it was a half hour before seven when they finished the food.

"Whew! That hit the spot."

She grinned as she packed the basket with the empty cartons. "Apparently, I have to take care of you and make sure you eat, *Mr. Rutherford*." She put emphasis on the end of the sentence, and he grinned

"Oh, I like the sound of that."

Jemma looked at him over her shoulder as she walked toward the clear windows. She immediately loved the view and that the office was up high. Will went to sit behind his desk, turning the swivel chair toward her. He liked how the dress looked against her skin, and he got erect.

"You look very pretty today, Jemma."

She turned his way with her eyes glowing. She went to the bookshelf that was adjacent to the windows, looking at the law books briefly. She leaned on the wall across from him with her hands folded in front of her.

"Thank you." He was leaning back in his chair with his legs open where she could see him raised at attention.

"Oh, no you don't, mister. I didn't come here for that!" she expressed to him, jerking her head toward his hard-on.

"What? I can't control a normal reaction." He shrugged casually, and she curled her lips. "Uh huh. I'm going to leave you to your work now that you're fed."

"You're not feeling the least bit antsy, sweetie? It's been damn near two weeks."

She let out a shuddering breath. Will saw her nipples strain against her dress.

"I just wanted to come feed you," she stated honestly.

Yeah, bet I can get her to change her mind, he said to himself. She lapped at her lips, and Will was glad he locked the door, especially since some heavy-duty sexing was about to go down.

"Lift up your dress. I want to see what you're wearing under it."

"You are not listening to me, Will."

RUTHERFORD'S WOMAN 2

"I heard everything you said. Now, less talking, more lifting."

"So bossy," she muttered, doing as he said. Jemma lifted up the thin dress to show a peach silk thong. She pressed her lips together when he motioned for her to turn around.

"Now, take it off," Will's voice had gotten deeper and husky; the rich, raspy sound turned her on.

She slowly tugged her undies down her legs and flung them toward Will with the tip of her shoe. He caught them in the air, brought them to his nose, and sniffed. She walked over to him, and he told her to bend over his desk with her butt facing him. She complied, and she started to breathe heavily when he lifted her dress to bear her ass. A low mewling sound escaped her lips when she felt his hands skim over the flesh in between her legs, and he parted her pulsating lips before sliding his tongue between them. She felt his tongue flutter over her glistening sex button, taking his time flicking and savoring her moist center; a wheezing noise filled the room when he slid two fingers inside her.

Between his tongue doing one thing and his sheathed fingers doing something else, Jemma's skin became hot, and she was begging him not to stop and indirectly moving against his digits to increase the friction. His free hand was roughly squeezing her butt cheeks, and her hands firmly held onto the edge of the wooden desk. Will sat back, unfastened his pants, and roughly took her by the waist. He settled her on him, hearing her sigh with delight. His legs were pressed together, and hers were spread open. Jemma braced her hands on his knees as she moved up and down on him. Will lifted her clothing so he could watch her wet, pretty vulva consume him with her slow actions.

"That's it right there. Don't you stop."

He rasped, reaching around to run his thumb up and down her clitoris. Jemma's eyes were closed, and her mouth was partly open as she switched to moving back and forth on him. Every time things got sexual with Will, it was always exciting and amazing. She couldn't imagine that nothing felt as satisfying as having him sex her up good, and she liked that he wasn't a selfish lover. A severe gasp erupted from her when he grabbed her hair and yanked her head back on his shoulder. His huge hands crept between her dress where he roughly kneaded and caressed her breasts; his fingers played with her hardened nipples. One of her hands curved around to cup his head, and the other one covered his hand that was touching her bosom. She continued to move on him so that his shaft was going in and out from tip to base.

"Oh God, Will," she whispered, feeling him lick the area behind her left ear.

"I know, baby. This shit feels good."

She let out a small laugh at his words. A creamy spasm escaped her when he started fondling her middle again. Even as her body was jerking from her orgasm, Will was far from climaxing, and Jemma knew she was in for a long ride when he indicated for her to take her time and make it last.

CHAPTER 5

It was the first day of the Diana Lake murder trial, and opening statements would begin the procedure. The amount of press had doubled outside the courtroom and officers had to help Michael and his family into the building. There was a strained yet electrifying mood in the air. The media knew this was the hottest story in the city, and they wanted to make sure nothing was missed on their part.

Michael knew the day was coming up and had gotten himself prepared for it, no matter how many restless nights and queasy stomach pains he had to endure. The people in the courtroom were waiting for the judge to arrive, and the gallery was filled with friends and family of the Lake and Vy families and other onlookers. The partners from Will's law firm were in attendance as well. Their presence didn't deter Will; he knew they were there to see how everything would go down and how he would conduct himself while representing the firm. It was going on nine in the morning, and Will looked at Michael, who was tapping his foot fretfully.

"It's going to be okay, Michael. Remember, just answer the questions simply. If you can, keep the answers short by saying *yes* or *no*. If you can't recollect, just say, 'I can't recall,'" Will said, patting his back.

He could tell Michael was super anxious and hoped the young man could keep it together.

"I got it, Mr. Rutherford. I have this knot in the pit of my stomach. I actually threw up this morning," Michael confided in Will who nodded. Michael had on tan trousers and a dress shirt to match. Will was wearing a black power suit with a red shirt and a black silk tie.

"All rise! The Honorable Judge Arroyo presiding." Everyone stood at the bailiff's words as a medium height Mexican man with brown hair walked in and sat down.

"Good morning to all," the judge said as he got settled in his seat. Greetings were returned, and he uncapped his pen.

"Are you ready, counselors?"

"Yes, Your Honor."

"Ms. Santiago, you may proceed."

Mr. and Mrs. Vy held hands as the prosecutor stood up and walked toward the jury box.

"Good morning, ladies and gentlemen of the jury. You are here today for one thing and one thing only…justice for Diana Lake. A young woman who was smart, bright, who brought joy to her family, and had aspired to have her own business. Sadly, those dreams won't come true because her life was prematurely ended by Michael Vy, a man who claimed to love and protect her. You're going to hear testimony from people who will say that they argued a lot. They were a cute couple. They had ups and downs, but why did he kill her? We don't know. We don't know what makes people tick, but Michael Vy got into a quarrel with the victim, and things got worse. Your only job is to seek justice for a woman who did nothing to deserve the ending she got. Be her advocate, and see that the right thing is done so her passing won't be in vain," Lori ended with that and went to go sit down.

Will stood up and buttoned his suit jacket. "Good morning. Ms. Santiago did a good job of presenting what she thinks happened between my client and Ms. Lake. She failed to mention that Mr. Vy has no criminal record; he doesn't even have a traffic ticket. My client is a generous man. He's given his time and money to several worthy charities, and he's an active member of the Boys and Girls Club. His relationship with the deceased wasn't perfect, but who has an affiliation without any problems? Those same testimonies that the ADA spoke of will also tell you that the two individuals cared and loved each other. The simple fact is there is no case here. There is no motive, no intent, and no reason for my client to have killed Ms. Lake. We do agree on one thing, and that is justice for Diana Lake. However it comes about, that should not include sending an innocent man to jail for a murder he didn't commit." Will sat down on that note, seeing the look of gratitude on Michael's face.

"Ms. Santiago, please call your first witness."

"The people called Detective Eric Polsen."

Will was making notes as she questioned the officer who was the first to arrive at the murder scene. Once she finished, Will stood and approached the bench.

"Officer Polsen, you testified that a 911 call came from Ms. Lake's neighbors at 10:17 a.m."

"Yes, that's right."

"And you had access to the apartment how?"

"The door was unlocked when I checked after I identified myself."

"In all your time on the force, how many murder scenes have you come across?"

"More than I can count," Officer Polsen said automatically.

"And how many have you seen where, after a person commits a crime, they clean up after themselves, they lock the door of an apartment, or they stay so the police can catch them?"

"Objection, Your Honor! Relevance?" Lori asked, standing up.

"This is in relation to my client's so-called state of mind and reasonable doubt, Your Honor," Will replied, looking at the judge.

"Overruled."

Lori sat down in a self-contained sulk, and Will turned back toward the officer.

"It is typical that when one commits a murder, they tend to flee right away to avoid being caught."

"Did you find it strange that my client was still there when you arrived?"

"I was shocked, yes."

"Was him being there the characteristic of a guilty man?" Officer Polsen swallowed before answering. "Well, no, but—"

"No further questions."

The judge gave the OK for the policeman to step down, and Ana called her next witness. "The state calls Mrs. Glenda Lake." The short woman made her way to the bench and was sworn in by the law officer.

"Mrs. Lake, how do you feel about Michael Vy?" Lori questioned the woman, standing close to the jury box.

"I think he's a fine young man. I love him like a son."

Lori made a face at that. "You love your daughter's killer like a son?"

"Objection, Your Honor!" Will boomed.

"Sustained. Watch it, Ms. Santiago," Judge Arroyo warned her.

"Sorry, I'll redirect."

Just as she was about to ask another question, the fire alarm went off in the building. The flashing lights and blaring sound overpowered the environment.

"Bailiff, go check to see if this is a drill," Judge Arroyo directed to the bulky guard. Will looked at the partners, who shrugged. Security rushed back into the courtroom and went to speak in the judge's ear.

"OK, the court will reconvene in two days. There's a small electrical fire in the basement, and we have to evacuate the premises."

Will said a quick word to Michael and his parents, and the entire building was soon emptied with the assistance of firefighters.

∾

Jemma was curled up on the leather couch in the employee lounge, trying to muster up the energy to get up and go home. She had ended up doing a double shift, and she was drained. After working over seventeen hours, all she wanted to do was sleep. Jemma had gotten off work at nine, and she kept telling herself five more minutes, then she'd get up and leave. That was twenty minutes ago, and she was still lying down. Phoebe walked in to get a drink of water, and she saw her friend still here.

"Hey, Jemma, get up, and go home," Phoebe prodded, gently shaking her arm.

"I am. Just resting my eyes for a second," she replied in a drowsy tone.

"Uh huh. If I come back and you're still here, I'm going to throw some cold water on you." Jemma didn't respond as she turned around on the couch.

Meanwhile, at the admissions counter, the desk clerk was listening to the CB radio from an incoming transmission.

"Dr. Reed, listen to this. Truck 134, please repeat last communication."

Dr. Reed was one of the attending physicians on call in the ER and listened to the message with a frown.

"MVA involving delivery truck and a school bus. At least eight EMT's are heading your way with five critical. ETA two minutes." Dr. Reed looked at Dr. Tripp, who was the pediatric attending doctor, and his eyes got big.

"Alright, you heard the man. Go prep the trauma rooms, and get crash carts ready. Dr. Langham call surgery, and tell them that we need a consult. Someone go check to see if Jemma is still here; it's all hands-on deck."

A minute hadn't passed before the paramedic doors opened, and a gurney was being wheeled in. Phoebe ran toward the break room with a pair of gloves in her hands to notify Jemma.

"Get up! Major trauma on the way from an MVA!"

Jemma sat up at her friend's urgent manner, blinking several times to get her bearings. She grabbed her stethoscope off the table and walked into the madness going on in the ER.

∼

"You did well for the first day," Dante said to Will, who was logging off his computer.

"Thanks, sir. It was pretty crazy with that fire."

"These things happen," Dante responded with a shrug. They left Will's office and headed toward the break room to get a cup of coffee. "What are you going to do now?"

"I was planning to stop by the Vy home to check on Michael."

Will and Dante stopped in their tracks when they saw a group of people hovered around the TV that was mounted on the wall in the lunchroom.

"What's going on, Fiona?" Will asked, and he looked at the TV when she pointed to it. The words "Breaking News" scrolled across the bottom of the screen.

"To repeat, a delivery truck for the Sky Hawk Logistics trucking company collided with a school bus that was making its way toward the Lincoln Park Zoo. We don't know if there are any casualties, but we were told that most of the children, including the truck driver, were taken to Mercy Heart Hospital. Please stay with us as we bring you continuous coverage of the unfolding story."

The news faded into a soft drink commercial, and the people in the room started to talk amongst themselves. Will excused himself with Dante and left the building after grabbing his jacket. He didn't know why, but he had a sense of urgency to go to Jemma's job after hearing about the accident from the newscaster.

~

"I don't care! We need all the O negative blood you have. Stat!" Jemma hung up with the blood bank, running back to the nine-year-old girl who was crying. Her leg was broken, she had a gash on her shoulder, and Dr. Tripp was using a portable ultrasound machine to check for internal bleeding.

"Ssh, you're going to be OK, sweetheart." Jemma injected ten ccs of morphine to numb the pain for when Dr. Tripp snapped the bone back in place.

"I want my mom!" the little girl screamed.

"We're going to call her. Let us take care of you."

She let out an ear-piercing scream when the bone was set, and Jemma quickly worked with the doctor to bind the leg. The girl got quiet, and they looked up to see she had passed out. Another physician worked on the rest of her body.

"Pulse is ninety. Orthopedics should be on the way down," Jemma told the doctor, who nodded.

"It looks like we're good here. Go help Langham with the driver in exam room three."

Jemma left as she ripped the plastic gloves off while heading to the specific room. Rushing down the hall, she saw two black tags on small bodies on gurneys and Jemma mentally shook the images from her mind. She had to stay focused and help save the patients that kept coming from the crash site. One of the teachers, Mrs. Stonewall, was crying as she paced the waiting area with disheveled and bloody clothes.

"Have you called the parents?" Jemma asked, pausing to assist the woman. "The school is doing it. I'm going to wait for them here," she mentioned, wringing her hands.

"Are you OK?" Jemma asked, looking at the blood on her neck. "Yes, I'm fine."

She walked into the room, donning new gloves. The driver of the delivery truck was singing the national anthem as Dr. Langham was feeling his neck for any injuries. Jemma got hit with a scent of vodka from the motorist, and she wrinkled her nose.

"You smell that? Pulse ox is ninety-two," she asked Evan. "Yep. I need a Chem seven and a CBC."

"Sir, can you squeeze my fingers?" Jemma asked the drunk, who belched loudly.

"I can do more than that, pretty lady."

She rolled her eyes and grabbed a syringe to draw some blood. "You want to order a C-spine?" Jemma asked Evan as she grabbed two IV bags.

"Yea, just to be on the safe side. It looks like he only has a damn broken wrist," Evan mumbled, taking the vitals. Jemma took off the neck brace and started an IV on the patient.

"He's not going anywhere for a while," Evan said, motioning toward the police who were waiting in the hall.

"You can go assist Dr. Turner," Dr. Langham said to Jemma, and she left to enter the next trauma. Just as she put on new gloves, the heart monitor started to beep rapidly.

"He's in V-fib, bag him!" Jemma ripped open the pediatric ambulation equipment and started to bag the little boy on the gurney as Gary was charging the defibrillator.

"Charging to two hundred. Clear!" Dr. Turner pushed the buttons on the paddles to administer the shock.

"Still no pulse," Jemma reported as she resumed the bagging.

"Charging to 250. Clear!" The machine didn't show a change, and she looked at Gary, who was looking how she felt. "Charge to three hundred. Clear!" Dr. Turner did another shock, and Gary looked at the equipment.

"Asystole."

"C'mon, little guy. Fight. Charge to 350. Clear!" Jemma lifted her hands and looked at the clock.

There had been no activity for over four minutes, and she went back to bagging. How did a simple field trip to the zoo turn into this? All because some irresponsible bastard decided to drink and drive. They continued to shock the lifeless body of the boy and administer life-saving measures. The nurses did not stop until the doctor had done all she could. Twenty minutes later, the steady beep of the machine made everyone in the room aware of what just happened.

"Dr. Turner, it's been over twenty-five minutes," Gary said, continuing the CPR. The older woman sighed and replaced the paddles on the defibrillator machine.

"Stop compressions. I'm calling it. Time of death... 12:52 p.m."

Gary disconnected the small green ambulation bag and stepped back. Jemma jumped when Dr. Turner angrily pushed the IV stand out of the way.

"More EMT's are coming. Go get ready," Dr. Turner said.

Jemma followed Gary out the room as they discarded the soiled gloves. They didn't say anything as they made their way back to the ambulance dock, hoping no other kids would succumb to their injuries.

∽

When Will got to the hospital, there was so much pandemonium in the emergency room, it made his head spin. Some of the children's parents who were involved in the accident were there, and they were understandably in a panic. There were twelve parents total, and their combined voice had raised the noise in the waiting area. He heard multiple conversations going on at once and knew they wanted answers right now.

"Why can't I see my daughter?"

"Who is in charge?"

"Where is that son-of-a-bitch driver?"

"Please let me see my son!"

The hospital security was being aided by some officers from the Chicago police department to help contain the angry, worried parents.

"Why can't someone tell us what's going on with our kids?" one father asked the desk clerk, who had a clipboard in her hand.

"Sir, the doctors, and nurses are working on the children, and they'll come out to let you know what's going on when they can."

"That's not good enough. I want to speak to whoever is in charge right now!" Will couldn't seem to stop himself from going over to confront the man.

"Sir, they're dealing with major trauma. Let them do their job!" Will roared at the man, who looked surprised for a second.

"Who the hell are you?" the father reacted, his face a mask of fury and worry.

"I know one of the nurses here, and I know they are doing everything they can to save your kids."

"Screw you, man! We have a right to know what the hell is going on!" The man yelled.

Will took his upper arm, growling in his ear, "You need to calm down. This is a serious situation, and these parents are already worried enough as it is. Stop making it worse."

The guy let out a shuddering exhale and nodded at Will, realizing that he wasn't making things better. Will understood the man was lashing out because he was concerned and didn't know what was going on behind the security doors. The TV was on, and it was reported that some of the other victims had been transported to the county hospital. He hoped those adolescents were well, and he couldn't imagine what the parents were going through. What if their children were in a different hospital than the one they were waiting at? That was something Will knew the parental units didn't want to consider, given the nature of the situation.

"Excuse me. I've just been asked to collect information regarding your family member like the color clothes they had on, hair and eye color, or any birthmarks. Please come and give it to me in an orderly fashion," the desk clerk announced and some of the parents rushed over to her. Just then, paramedics rushed through the emergency doors, and the parents looked on in horror.

"Little girl crushed by the impact of the truck. Internal injuries. BP is 90/60, pulse ox is 77. She was in cardiac arrest, and we shocked her twice to bring her back," the paramedics read off the patient's vitals as Dr. Reed put on fresh gloves.

"Okay, let's move her to room five."

"All the traumas are filled," one nurse let him know. The little girl's pulse started to fall, and the doctor cursed.

The guy who was going back and forth with Will looked at the EMT's and gasped. "Ella? That's my daughter!"

"Let them work on her."

"We need a thoracotomy kit now! We're going to have to do this in the hall," Dr. Reed said, pulling out a scalpel as she went into cardiac arrest.

Jemma poured iodine on the girl, and Will was in awe as he

observed her working. He watched as Jemma positioned the rib spreader so the physician could get access to the child's heart. They didn't have a defibrillator machine so it would have to be done manually. She had been down for almost two minutes, and Jemma watched as Dr. Reed tried to get to her heart.

"Dammit, my hands are too big. Jemma…"

She reached into the chest cavity, and once she could feel the heart, she started to move her hands in a wave-like motion, and soon, they had a heartbeat.

"Okay, let's get her to surgery stat! Someone call up to the O.R." Jemma hopped on the gurney as it was being pushed toward the elevators. The unruly man walked to the registration desk; his breath came out in uneven pants.

"T-that is my d-daughter. I need to see her," he requested in a shaky, low voice

"Take the elevator to the fourth floor. Someone up there will show you where to go." The man rushed away, and Will sighed astoundingly.

What he'd just seen was incredible, and he hoped the actions were enough to save the little girl's life. Once the patient had been whisked away to the operating room, Jemma warily walked back down to the ER. It seemed like things had calmed down on the main floor. The parents had been allowed to see their kids, and she knew the doctors were taking their time, explaining each injury. She was at the nurse's station, signing off on charts and looked to the left to see the mother of the deceased little boy crying as she bent over the small, sheet covered body. She quickly looked away and said a prayer for the family. Dr. Reed and the charge nurse walked up to her with grim looks on their faces.

"Jemma, we got this. You did a double then this trauma came in. Go home," the doctor said, taking the charts from her.

"Take four days off to recharge your batteries," the charge nurse said, and Jemma mumbled her thanks.

As she gathered her things from her locker, she paused to collect herself. Of course, this wasn't her first child related ordeal, but to get it back-to-back like this was something else. Jemma felt terrible for those parents of the kids who hadn't made it, knowing this would alter their lives forever. She had gotten a ride to work, so she'd have to take the bus. That was probably the best alternative since she didn't have the energy to drive. She headed toward the exit and was surprised to see Will waiting for her. Jemma let out an appreciative smile, walked over to him and he gave her a tight hug.

"Are you okay?"

"No," she answered honestly, her voice quivering.

"Let's get you home."

~

JEMMA HAD FALLEN asleep as soon as she was settled in Will's car. He glanced at her as he was driving on the expressway. He knew she was exhausted, and he wanted to get her to bed as soon as possible. He was taking her to his house where he could make sure she would get the proper rest. Finally pulling up to the garage, he got out and went to get Jemma out the car by carrying her inside. He took her upstairs with no problem and placed her on the bed. Will left to go turn on the shower after taking off his jacket. He sat next to her and began to take her shoes and scrubs off. He took her ponytail down and gently massaged her scalp.

"Jemma, wake up, baby. Time to take a quick shower." She groaned in her sleep, and he shook her again.

"Jemma?" She opened one eye, and he chuckled.

"Will?"

"I've got a nice shower waiting for you."

"I'm so tired," she slurred.

"I know, love. But after you shower and eat, you can sleep all you want."

She grudgingly went to the restroom, and she removed her underwear and stepped into the glass-encased space. He went downstairs and made Jemma a hearty turkey sandwich with a cup of veggie soup.

By the time she got out, he was upstairs with a food tray for her. Jemma had left some clothes there and had on a cotton chemise.

"Okay, eat up." She sat, looking at him with half-closed eyelids. "I'm not really hungry, Will."

"Yeah? Well, you still need to eat something. Now, are you going to do it, or do I have to force you?"

"No. Jeez."

After consuming the food, she thanked him, and he took the tray back down to the kitchen. When Will got back to his bedroom, Jemma was passed out sleep, and he ran a thumb over her cheek after covering her with a light blanket.

CHAPTER 6

Two days later, Will had walked into his office, placing the umbrella on the floor in a corner. He'd left a note for Jemma who had slept on and off the last two days. It was looking like it was going to be a rainy day judging from the clouds that were forming over the lake. It was 6:30 a.m., and he saw a manila envelope sitting on his desk. He opened it and read the content of the paternity test.

"You gotta be kidding me!" Dante walked into Will's office, holding a cup of coffee.

"You ready for court, Will?" He didn't answer Mr. Fry, and the elderly man's eyebrows went up. "Will?"

"I'm sorry, sir. Yes, I'm ready," he excused himself and went to the copy room where he made a duplicate of the paper.

He called an express courier service to have the copy sent to the ADA's office. He necessarily didn't have to share this information with Lori, but he wanted to be courteous and let her know she was about to lose the case. After dealing with the messenger, Will jumped on his computer and pulled up the website to look for public records.

Meanwhile, Jemma was walking into her apartment and had rushed to her bedroom. She had woken up as soon as she heard Will leave and had called a cab after reading his note. She knew he was due back in court today, and she wanted to be there for him to show her support since she couldn't attend the first day. She hurried and packed her overnight bag since she was going to go back to Will's house later. Jemma grabbed a white blouse and skirt from her closet and went to go look for some shoes.

～

"Mr. Vy, can I speak to you for a second?" Will asked when he caught up with the husband and wife in the hallway of the courthouse as they were about to walk into the room. The rain had started to fall a half hour ago, and they had a few minutes to spare before court started.

"Of course."

Mr. Vy followed Will to an empty corner, and he looked at the lawyer. Will was donning a slate gray suit with a white shirt and a dark purple tie.

"I need to ask you a question. It's an intrusive and personal one, but I need an answer," Will let him know, and the man frowned.

"What is it?"

"Have you ever had a sexual relationship with Diana?" Mr. Vy blanched at the question and placed a hand on the stone wall for support.

"No! What the hell type of question is that?"

"I'm sorry, sir. I didn't mean any disrespect, but I needed to know."

"I love my wife and would never cheat on her. Why would you ask me that?"

"I received some last-minute information, and I needed to rule you out. It might be what we need to help your son walk away a free man."

Mr. Vy blinked away the tears that sprouted in his eyes, and Will patted him on the back reassuringly.

"Do you have any other male relatives living close by?"

"No, my uncle lives in Arizona, and he's in a nursing home. Why do you ask?"

"All in due time, Mr. Vy."

They walked into the somber room, and Jemma was able to get inside before the doors closed, knowing once they were, no one would be allowed entrance while court was in session.

Will felt a sharp awareness at the back of his neck. He turned toward the gallery and searched the audience until he spotted Jemma sitting in the back row on the left. He was truly surprised to see her, but he was glad she was there. A small part of him was thrilled that she would be able to see him in authentic action unlike the mock situation she attended in school. She waved at him, and he winked at her. The judge walked in ten minutes later, and everyone stood.

"My apologies for the tardiness. Ms. Santiago, you may call your first witness."

"The state calls Michael Vy."

Will gave him an encouraging nod, and he got up to walk to the witness stand with his head held high.

"Mr. Vy, how long have you known Ms. Lake?"

"Since high school. We had a lot of classes together, and we ended up hanging out a lot."

"And when did the relationship get romantic?"

"The summer before senior year."

"Did you love her?" Lori asked with her hands clasped in front of her.

"Yes. I was going to ask her to marry me."

"So, why didn't you? Was it because the spark had left the relationship or because you had a change of heart?" Lori asked, slowly pacing the floor.

"Objection, Your Honor!" Will said loud and clear, his voice booming off the walls of the place. The sounds of the heavy rain could be heard hitting the three oval-shaped windows.

"Withdrawn. We have signed statements from witnesses that say you two argued a lot and some escalated to screaming matches. What was the nature of those arguments?"

"It was a lot of different things. She said I wasn't spending enough time with her, and I wasn't dedicated to our relationship."

"Did you agree?"

"No. Everything I was doing, I did for us. I wanted us to have a nice house and be financially established."

"Tell us about the day you found her in her apartment."

Michael hesitated before going on; he glanced at Will and knew his lawyer was there for him.

"I had been trying to call her for days, but she hadn't returned my calls. So, I went over to her place and used my key to get in. I walked in and saw her in all that blood. I didn't know she was dead. I grabbed her arms to shake her to wake her up."

"And that was the first time you went to her apartment that day?"

"Yes," Michael answered strongly.

"So, how do you explain her neighbor hearing you two argue a week before she died and hours before her death?"

"I admit, we did argue that first time, but whoever she was talking to in her apartment on that day, it wasn't me."

"Ah! So, you're saying it was another man?"

"No, I didn't say that. I—"

"Suppose Ms. Lake," Lori cut Michael off, "did feel like you weren't as committed to her, and she found another man to spend time with; that certainly would upset you." Lori was standing in front of him, one hand resting on the oak bench.

"Objection! Is there a question here?" Will asked from the table, his pen gripped in his hand.

"Get to the point, Ms. Santiago."

"Do you think there was another man in her life?"

"No."

"You just admitted that your relationship was strained. You were arguing, fighting, and not around a lot. If there was a new guy around, that's motive to do her harm, isn't it?"

"I did not hurt Diana; I loved her!"

"And yet her neighbor heard arguing hours before her death. That doesn't sound like love. No further questions, Your Honor." Will gave Lori the side eye as she went to go sit down and he stood up.

"The defense has no questions for Mr. Vy." Michael looked at Will with question in his eyes, and Will slightly shook his head.

"You may step down, young man," Judge Arroyo said to Michael.

Will had enough of the ADA's questions and her intent to twist the events around to win her case.

"The defense calls Tanya Powers." Diana's neighbor was a middle-aged white woman who was wearing a bad wig and had been the one who called the cops during both verbal incidents.

"How long had you been living next door to Ms. Lake?" Will dived right into his line of questioning as soon as she was sworn in.

"About a year."

"Were you friends with her?"

"We greeted each other in passing, but that was it."

"Have you ever seen my client at the apartment building before?" Will asked, pointing at Michael.

"Yes. One day, Diana introduced me to him."

"So, the week before the death, you told the police you heard Ms. Lake and my client arguing. How did you know it was him?"

"I was on my way out to the store, and I saw him leave her apartment that day. He slammed the door after him and took the stairs to leave the building."

"How was he when you saw him? Upset? Cool?"

"Objection, he's leading the witness."

"Sustained. Move on, Mr. Rutherford," the judge ordered.

"OK, so the day of Ms. Lake's passing, you again told the officer that you heard arguing and that it was my client."

"Correct."

He placed his hands in his pockets and pinched his lips.

"Did you see Mr. Vy enter or leave her apartment that day?"

"Well, no, but—"

"So, because of what you previously witnessed, you assumed it was my client. When, in fact, you can't say for sure because you didn't see him that day. What you heard could've been a loud TV. It could've been a family member, a co-worker. Given all those possibilities and the fact that you didn't see Michael Vy that day, are you positive that it was him you heard talking to Ms. Lake on the day she died?"

Tanya looked away as she considered his question, her face showing uncertainty. The room was apprehensively quiet as they waited for her to answer.

"Miss. Powers, please answer the question," the judge prodded lightly.

"No, but—"

"No further questions," Will interrupted Tanya's further explanation. A quiet murmur flowed through the courtroom.

Lori had no questions for the neighbor, and she stepped down.

"The defense calls Tilda Vy."

Michael's cousin looked up startled and glanced at her uncle and aunt before taking the stand. Her heart pounded fast. Jemma was excited, yet nervous about what was going on. She was so proud of Will, and she knew it was inappropriate, but she was so charmed by Will at that moment. Seeing him all lawyer-y, being comfortable in his element was such a turn on!

"How did you know the victim?" Will asked, pulling out the paper he got that morning and put it face down on the table.

"We used to hang out in high school."

"And you two kept in touch over the years?"

"Yes."

"Did you know where she lived?" Will was asking simple questions, and Tilda felt at ease.

"Yes. We used to go over there several times to play cards and stuff."

"Did you have a key?" Will asked, standing in front of the table with one hand in his pocket. Tilda didn't answer; she licked her lips and cleared her throat.

"Ms. Vy, did you have a key to Diana Lake's apartment?"

"Yes, I had a key." Michael looked at his parents in confusion.

The judge banged his gavel to quiet the low talking in the room. "Order!"

Michael was wondering the same thing some other people were thinking. Why *did* Tilda have a key to Diana's apartment?

"Now, when I spoke to the Lake family, her mother told me she had the spare key, so why did you have one?"

Tilda took a deep breath to answer, but Will stopped her. "That's OK; we'll come back to that. Did you know Ms. Lake was pregnant?" Will asked, silently daring her to say no.

Michael sat up in his chair in eagerness. Jemma's eyes bounced between Will and Tilda.

"Yes, I knew Diana was pregnant."

More droning passed through the gallery, and the judged bashed his gavel again. "Order in the court!"

Will walked back to the table where he grabbed the paper containing the paternity test results.

"Judge Arroyo, I have here the results of the paternity test from the fetus of the deceased. With the court's permission, I'd like Ms. Vy to read the highlighted part," Will said, holding up the sheet of paper.

"Objection! The state has no knowledge of this report and questions the authenticity of it!" Lori stood up, her face growing red.

"Counselors approach the bench," Judge Arroyo commanded as he covered the microphone as Will carried the report and another document with him.

"Your Honor, the defense is trying to—"

"I heard your objection the first time, Ms. Santiago. Mr. Rutherford?" The judge read the paperwork over the top of his glasses as Will was clarifying.

"As you can see by the State of Illinois seal and notary with the medical examiner's signature, this is the original document I received. I also have here a signed receipt of delivery of the copy I had couriered to the ADA's office this morning with a timestamp and signature," Will spoke as he handed the judge the receipt, and he looked at it.

"Is there a Kasey Archer at your office?"

Lori closed her eyes, and she nodded. "She's a clerk, Your Honor."

"I suggest you find competent people who can present important correspondences to you regarding your cases. I'll allow the results." Lori walked away, and Will handed the paper to Tilda.

"Can you read the highlighted part out loud, please?"

"The blood sample and mouth swab taken from the unborn nine-week-old fetus do not match the swab sample taken from donor Michael Vy. Probability match is one percent. The analyzed test does share the same Y chromosome as the alleged father," Tilda finished reading and gave it back to Will.

"Did you understand what you just read?"

"My cousin wasn't the father."

Michael closed his eyes, and the Vy family squeezed each other's hand while tears ran down Mrs. Lake's face. Will could understand the different feelings the two families were experiencing upon hearing the stunning news, but he had a purpose and a job to do.

"And what about the last part?"

"N-no. I don't understand what it said," Tilda answered truthfully.

"In a nutshell, the baby wasn't Michael's, but it was fathered by a male relative."

Will walked closer to the bench and read her eyes, knowing he was about to expose her secret. He didn't want to, and it wasn't his right, but his first and only obligation was to Michael and proving his innocence.

"Your birth name isn't Tilda, is it?" He could see the fear and dread in her gaze, and she briefly closed her eyes. She looked at her family, mouthing *I'm sorry* to Michael.

"No, I was born Timothy Vy," Tilda announced with pride, her head held up high. The judge had to strike the gavel several times to get a resemblance of order when the room erupted after her last words.

"Another outburst, and I will clear everyone out!"

Will couldn't tell how the jury was feeling since their faces were impartial and void of any emotion. He waited until the spectators settled down and for Tilda to compose herself.

"Diana was carrying your child, wasn't she?"

"Yes," she replied in a low voice.

"Can you tell us what happened?"

"Diana was going to leave Michael; she wasn't happy with him. I wanted us to run away together after she told me about the baby, but she wanted to tell him about us. I thought if they did talk, they'd end up back together again. We fell in love, and we wanted to be together. It just happened, and we didn't plan it. Diana didn't judge me or the choices I made about my life."

Will walked back to the table and looked at Michael, who was shaking his head.

"What happened when Diana died?" Will asked softly, disbelieving how things were unfolding.

"It was me the neighbor heard Diana arguing with that day. I was going to leave town that night, and I wanted her to come with me, but she kept insisting on speaking with Michael first. She kept saying it was the right thing to do. We were disagreeing, and I tried to grab her arm. It wasn't to cause harm, but it was more to talk some sense into her. She jerked away from me, fell back, and hit her head on the wooden TV stand. When she didn't get up, I left the apartment... I don't know why. I was scared. I didn't know she had died; I just thought she was unconscious. I-I never wanted her to die. It was an accident."

Will sighed, nodded, and looked at Michael, who had tears in his eyes.

"Your Honor, given the testimony from Ms. Vy, I motion to dismiss the charges against my client," Will said as he was writing something.

"Ms. Santiago, any objections?"

"No," she answered after a slow minute, blowing out a heavy breath.

"Granted the circumstances of that we've just heard, I have no reason to deny Mr. Rutherford's request. The charges against Michael Vy are hereby dropped and dismissed. You are free to go, Mr. Vy."

Jemma watched as the courtroom exploded in cheers, questions, and confusion. She saw Will approached by two men, who whispered something in his ear. His client and his parents hugged Will with relief and gratitude on their faces. She noticed that Tilda had slipped off the stand and hurriedly left. Reporters were outside in the hall, and when the Vy and Lake families stepped out, the camera lights flickered like sparks, and microphones were thrust into their faces. There were several media personalities shouting off boisterous questions at Michael. Jemma had lost sight of Will in all the media frenzy, so she left the building and headed toward the parking lot.

CHAPTER 7

Will stood under the hot flow of the shower in his house. He was content with staying in the heated, misty space because it was very soothing and with the two shower heads going, he felt the stress and tension slowing being withdrawn from him. He was beyond elated that he'd won his case as were the partners.

After the Vy family had given a brief statement and he had ushered them out the building, Will stopped by the office, and he got more compliments from some people at the office, including Fiona. He had met briefly with Shane and Dante and had answered their questions patiently, liking the absorbed engrossed look on their faces. They had let him go home early and told him to take the rest of the week off to celebrate and get a short period of rest. He had given Fiona the rest of the week off too. His ever-efficient legal secretary suggested that it be a paid leave, and he had agreed to it with a good-humored smile.

Will had driven home in the buckets of rain that was coming down. The traffic was unbearable with the weather condition. Because he was upstairs, he didn't hear Jemma pull up in the driveway. It was only 4:30 p.m., but it appeared to be later than that with the precipitation. She turned the car off and put her purse into her overnight bag. She didn't have a jacket and had forgotten her umbrella at home, and she knew she would be soaked once she got out the vehicle. Bracing herself, she exited the Jeep, gasped and let out a tiny squeal as the heavy drops hit her clothes and skin. She let herself in with the key, dropped the bag by the door, and stepped out the soggy high heel shoes.

Jemma didn't see Will downstairs, so she trotted up the carpeted stairs and went into the dark bedroom. The bathroom room door was open, and she could hear the shower going. Will's body was almost invisible through the glass door from the steam circulating in the oblong space. Jemma lightly tapped the glass with her fingernails as to not startle him.

"Hey, Will. I just wanted to let you know I was here."

She didn't have time to think before the door was slid open, and she was hauled inside.

"Will! I'm—" he cut her words off by kissing her mouth.

It started her and continued to be a good, long mating of lips and tongues. The thought of being fully dressed soon left her mind. Jemma wrapped one arm around his neck and cupped his face with the free hand, moaning in her throat. Her white blouse became transparent from the hot water, and he could see the black lace bra through the material.

Will's big hands went to her waist and pulled down the black polyester skirt, which plopped on the floor in a drenched heap. He stepped back to take in her black garter belt and matching thong. He loved seeing the lacelike material hug her hips and curves; the color looked fantastic against her skin hue. Jemma didn't say anything when he ripped open her blouse. That action did something to her, and she brought his head down and urgently kissed him again.

Will fondled the curvatures of her behind, pushing her middle toward his protruding manhood. When he picked her up and held her against the wall, she opened her legs for his stature, and he gave her a predatory look. Jemma gasped and threw her head back when he pulled the material of her bra down, and he took a nipple into his mouth. Her hair was in a loose bun on top of her head, but a few damp pieces managed to escape and plaster against her face. She didn't mind that there was a two hundred pound plus profoundly aroused man holding her up. From what he was doing with his mouth, it was causing sweet, wonderful flutters to ripple up and down her body, and she didn't want the feeling to end. Will was eye-level with her succulent bosom, and he took his time licking the swells of them with his tongue before lapping the swollen buds. Jemma's fingernails were buried in the muscles in the back of his neck, but that didn't bother Will.

The pounding between her legs was literally making her ache, and she whispered "please, Will" in his ear. Her inner flesh automatically spasmed.

"*Please* what?" he asked, sucking on her left nipple. He was in the middle of something, and she was disrupting things.

"Fuck me," she replied, and he lifted his head to look at her.

Will wasn't shocked by what she'd said. In fact, it made him all hot that she had a potty mouth on her. To answer, he hooked his arms under her legs and eased inside her wetness until he was completely buried inside. Jemma embraced him, moaning softly as he started to move her up and down on him. Will started slowly until she was comfortable with the feeling then he began to increase the motion. His feet were firmly braced, making it easy for him to control the pace. Throaty, feminine groans were ripped from her throat. The sounds of balls slapping skin were bouncing off the walls of the enclosure. Jemma's back kept hitting the wall with each thrust, and he hoped he wasn't hurting her. Will could tell when she had an orgasm by the shaking of her body and her labored panting. Will had her thighs gripped hard as he continued to pound in her. Jemma was not upset when the touch got firmer.

"Dammit!" he said in a tough voice, flexing for one last powerful lunge when he came inside her. Jemma felt like she was floating on a cloud when he settled her on unsteady feet, unsnapping her bra. Her back was still pressed against the tiled wall, and Will's hands were on her waist when he bent down and placed a soft peck on her mouth.

"We're just getting started," he said against her puffy lips, and those four words got her going again.

Once she removed her garter belt and undies, she quickly washed with her loofah and the body wash that was on the shower caddy. Will reached for the big towel outside the glass door, and he dried them both off. He took her hand and pulled her into the room where he steered her onto the king size bed. Will crawled over her body and kissed her again. Jemma reclined to lie in the middle of the mattress. Her hands ran over the muscled slopes and angles of his damp torso as her nails scraped across his flat areolas. She loved his wide shoulders and the slimness of his body.

He leaned back and started to kiss his way down her chest and stomach. The air of the room caused the tips of her breasts to tighten, and her skin tingled when he licked the shape of her belly button. Once Will got down to her lower area, he licked his lips before diving between her open legs. She didn't know why, but Jemma could hear Will tasting and slurping on her, and that was so intoxicating to her. She cupped the back of his head as she rubbed against his swirling flesh, biting her lips, and her free hand caressing her right tit. Will felt himself getting hard again while he was stabbing his tongue inside her delicious opening. She had a flowery scent and a scrumptious taste. He honestly would be okay to just lie there and devour Jemma until she couldn't take it anymore.

However, his prick had other plans that would cause satisfaction on both parts. Jemma's mouth became dry from the open-mouth, hoarse cries, and she arched her back when Will gave her another shattering climax. Will sat up in a hurry and used one hand to direct his shaft to enter her again. Jemma let out a pleased sigh at the intrusion. His hands were braced on either side of her, and he leisurely prodded his stiffness in and out her tight heat.

She couldn't see his face in the dimness, but she knew that his eyes were open, and he was looking at her. Jemma didn't feel exposed or vulnerable by the stare. This felt so right, and she didn't want to be anywhere else. Her place was beside Will; it always was and would be. Will lowered himself so that their chests were touching. His breath brushed against her ear as he thrust deep into his woman. She ran loving hands down his tight back and moved down to squeeze his firm backside. Will lifted her left leg higher and buried himself deeper inside Jemma.

"I love you, Will," she said in a heartfelt whimper with her open lips pressed against his cheek. With a flick of his wrist, he had taken down her hairdo and ran his fingers through the soft strands.

"I love you, baby. Jesus, stop doing that before you make me come," he returned as he increased his tempo.

She squeezed her tendons around him, and he groaned. "Doing what?"

"You're milking me, and that shit feels good." She let out a cheeky smile and took his earlobe into her mouth. Will grabbed her hands and held them above her head. Their fingers interlocked.

"You feel so fucking good. I love how your tight pussy feels around me." All she could do was release shaken breaths with each deep push.

"You're mine, Jemma."

"I know, Will. Keep going."

"You're going to come for me?"

She moaned a "yes" with the syllables drawn out and her fingers clutching his tighter.

"That's right. This is mine!" Will rasped in her ear as they both had explosive ejaculations.

He weakly climbed off Jemma, got behind her and wrapped a hand around her stomach. Jemma could feel his pulse beating unsteadily as they were trying to regulate their heartbeats. Her head was pillowed on his bicep with their left hands still interlocked. They didn't bother to cover their naked bodies. The room was cool, but there was immense warmth coming from their post-coitus bodies.

"Are you OK?" he asked, his right hand resting on her hip.

"I'm fine, sweetie. Congratulations on your case. I'm so happy for you." Will meekly smiled at her words since he knew she meant it, and they felt valuable coming from her.

"Thank you, Jemma."

"You were so professional and efficient. If I ever need a lawyer, you're my guy."

"I better be," he said. His nose buried in her neck to inhale her fragrance.

"Are you tired, Will?"

"No, just basking in the sexual high." She brought his hand to her mouth and kissed his fingers.

"What happens now? Do you get another case?"

"The partners told me to take a few days off, and I'm giving the Vy family some time to process what happened today, but I'll probably get another client or two."

"I know they're relieved how it went down. I feel bad for his cousin," Jemma stated sincerely.

"Yeah. I'll ask about Tilda when I speak to Michael. Speaking of efficient, you were splendid at the hospital with everything that was going on. You probably saved that little girl's life."

"I hope so," she replied with a sigh. "I was going to call up there and find out if the surgery went OK."

"Would you think it's inappropriate if I told you watching you work got me all horny?"

She shook her head with a tender smile. "No. I was thinking the same thing today in the courtroom."

"Great minds, huh?"

Will snuggled closer to her, and they lay together in contentment and harmony. It was still raining hard, and the house shook when thunder struck.

"Do you have any candles?" she asked sleepily, turning to face Will.

"They're somewhere in the kitchen. Are you hungry?"

"No, I'm fine for right now, honey."

He touched her cheek, and she turned toward his touch. "I'm glad you came to see me in court today."

"I wouldn't have missed it, Will. I wanted to show my support. You should be pleased with the work you did."

"I am, Jemma. I'm just glad an innocent kid was saved."

"You're a good man, Will," she said just before she kissed him unhurriedly.

"And you're a great woman," he retorted, curling his right hand around her butt.

"So, we're off the next few days... whatever shall we do?" Jemma asked in between loveable pecks, and she felt him get semi-erect against her thigh.

"Well, I'm relaxing in bed. I don't know what you're going to do." She chuckled and pinched his shoulder.

"Ow!" He swatted her ass, and she yelped.

"Mmm, do that again," she mentioned, curling against him, her breasts flattened against his firm chest.

"I gotta tell you... I love this freaky side of you. You're talking dirty and encouraging spankings. We need to explore this."

Jemma sat up and pushed him on his back before sitting on top of him. Will's hands were resting on her folded legs, and she had her hands on his shoulder blades, looking down at his shape.

"So, you'd be open to us using handcuffs, whips and chains, and popsicles?"

It took Will a minute to process the question because she was biting and teasing certain parts of his chest, and he ran his hands up her back; his skin was overly sensitive and sexually humming.

"Wait, why did you mention popsicles? What are you going to do with them?" Jemma bent down and told him exactly how she would use the cold dessert, all the while she was slowly stroking his rigid penis behind her that was bouncing against her butt cheeks. It was powerful yet gratifying that she had caused him to pant and thrust himself into her soft hand.

"That is fucking sexy! I'm getting a box next time I go to the store."

Jemma let out a girly laugh and gave him a quick peck. "Relax baby."

She ran her tongue from his throat down to the bottom of his six-pack stomach. He inhaled sharply and grabbed the comforter when he felt her lick the tip of the delicate head of his shaft. She settled on her knees and took her time with him as she took his yummy cock into her mouth. Jemma was skillfully moving her head up and down his package and deep throating the hell out of him, and Will was loving every damn second of it.

With the sloppiness and maneuvering between his shaft and balls, he was on the cusp of a huge release, especially when she kept tweaking her tongue on the underside of the enlarged top. He grabbed her head and guided her movements, so she could keep the up and down gesture. Will let out a manly hiss when she added her hands to the blow job.

"Shit, Jemma!"

She was nonstop with her task; her own breathing turned into lustful puffs when he reached between her legs and started to finger her. Will's leg began to shake on the bed, and he felt like he would split in two when he finally bust a huge nut, not seeing the wicked stare that she gave him.

"You're so naughty," he let her know in a low, thick pitch.

He had maneuvered them, so they were resting on the pillows, and he pulled her so she was laying on his chest. They ended up falling asleep in that position. The last thing Jemma saw before closing her eyes was that the clock had just turned to 7:00 p.m. It was an on and off sleep because they'd get some rest and then wake up, feeling aroused and in heat. For the next few hours, it was sleep... doggy style... sleep... sixty-nine position... napping... reverse cowgirl... power nap... spoon style. After that last time, Will was down for the count, and Jemma had her eyes closed with a fulfilled smirk on her face.

∽

THE NEXT MORNING, after Jemma had taken a much-needed scorching shower, she had put on one of his undershirts after grooming herself and walked out the room. Will was still asleep, and she figured he could use the extra rest since he had put in long, overtime hours working on his case. After moving her bag and shoes that were by the front door, she headed toward the kitchen to make breakfast. The rain had stopped, but there was still an overcast outside. She opened the fridge and saw that it was fully stocked. Jemma gathered ingredients to make waffles and turned on the radio.

Upstairs, Will rolled over on his back and let out a loud yawn as he opened his eyes. He heard music coming from downstairs, and he sat up on his elbows. Will didn't see Jemma in the room, and he climbed out the bed, surprised that he could walk after their sexual interludes from last night and into the morning. He took a quick shower, brushed his teeth, threw on a pair of white and green striped pajama pants with no shirt, and made the bed before going downstairs.

Jemma was munching on an orange slice, bopping her head to James Brown's "Living in America" while she checked on the waffles that were cooking. He walked up behind Jemma and wrapped his sturdy arms around her.

"Hey, good morning," she said with a smile, turning to kiss his cheek.

"Good morning, beautiful. I see you're cooking up a storm in here."

"It's just a light breakfast. I thought you'd still be asleep. I was going to bring you breakfast in bed," she said to him as he reached for a fruit slice.

"You weren't there beside me," he declared as if that was enough.

He pushed her hair aside and nibbled on her neck. Jemma closed her eyes and leaned back into him, reaching around to feel his butt. The doorbell rang just as he touched her nipples that were pressing against the shirt.

"Who the hell is that?" he growled, heading toward the door after he gave them a quick pinch, and Jemma flung the kitchen towel at him. Will was stunned to see his grandmother standing on his doorstep with a uniformed man holding an umbrella over her head.

CHAPTER 8

"Hello, William."

"Grandmother." He stepped back to let her in, watching as she entered his home. "What are you doing here? And by here, I mean *Illinois*."

She clutched her cane in one hand and her purse in the other. She wore a rose-colored swing coat adorned with gold buttons and a pearl brooch that was pinned above her left breast.

"I came to commend you on your case." Will frowned at that.

"You flew all the way here to do that when you could've called?" he asked, not believing her words. She really was the last person he wanted to talk to, especially after what she admitted the last time they spoke.

"Aren't you going to offer me a seat?"

He let out an exasperated breath and jerked his head. "Right this way."

He led her into the living room where she sat on the couch. "I'll be right back." He returned to the kitchen as Jemma was turning off the waffle iron.

"My grandmother is here," he told Jemma without preamble.

"Mona is here?"

"Yes."

"Oh. I'll give you some privacy."

"No, you're coming with me." He grabbed her hand, but she drew it back.

"I need to go put on more clothes," she told him. Will looked at her, seeing the t-shirt come to the middle of her thighs.

"You're fine, sweetie. Besides, I have a feeling she won't be here long." He squeezed her hand reassuringly, and they walked into the other room. Mona was flabbergasted to see Jemma with Will; the younger girl's face showed unease at her lack of clothing.

"Good morning, Mrs. Rutherford."

"Morning, Ms. Alden. Will, I didn't know you had a guest."

"Well, that's generally why people call ahead first," he replied tersely, and Jemma looked at him, surprised by his tone.

"Will!"

"You're still mad. I get it. In addition to offering my praise, I actually came here to apologize for my actions ten years ago," Mona said, looking at the couple.

"An apology and congratulations in one day? What's really going on? You never say you're sorry about anything." Will asked as Jemma was staring at Mona. Of course, she had aged over the years, but she appeared fine with a healthy glow.

"Are you okay health-wise, Mrs. Rutherford?" He stared at Jemma sharply then turned to look at his grandmother.

"Yes, I'm fine, except for the occasional arthritis."

They didn't say anything as Mona sighed, and she fidgeted with the pearl handle of her walking device. Will was especially speechless since he'd never seen his grandma like that.

"You were right, Will. About what you said… about ending up alone. I have employees, but when they go home, it's utterly quiet. I have no one to talk to. No one to sit and relax with. You probably won't believe me, but I did love Joshua. I-I was just set in my ways, and it drove him away. I don't blame him for leaving. I just wanted to let you know I'm sorry for what I did, and I hope you both can forgive me."

Jemma let out a small grin and glanced at Will, who was sitting on the arm of the sofa chair, and he didn't say anything for a long time. He didn't like being at odds with Mona given her age and distance they lived from each other. He went over to her, hunched down, and gave her a tight hug.

"You're such a crazy old lady." Mona laughed at that and wiped her tears away.

"So, I've been told."

"We were just about to sit down to eat breakfast. Would you care to join us?" Jemma asked, looking back and forth between Will and Mona.

"No, thank you. I'm on my way back to the airport."

"Where are you going?"

"To see your brother. I've never been on a military base before."

"Oh, I don't know about that. You might want to—"

"I've already spoken to Robert, and he knows I'm coming. I had to get security clearance and everything. How exciting is that?"

Jemma coughed to cover up her giggle, and she watched the older lady approached her and tenderly patted her cheek.

"You are a special woman. Take care of my grandson."

"Yes, ma'am," she promised, blinking back the tears in her eyes.

Jemma had told herself a long time ago that she didn't care what Mona thought about her and hadn't cared about her unfair attitude, but she felt like the book had been closed at Mona's apology, and she internally felt better about it. Will walked his grandmother to the door as she went back to the kitchen. She took a sip of coffee, still shaken by Mona's words. Jemma never thought Mona would admit that she was wrong or apologize for her actions. She hoped this would be the thing to restart Will's relationship with Mona. Jemma was leaning against the counter when Will walked in with one hand in his pants pocket.

"Are you OK?" she asked after giving him a long hug.

"Yes. She's going to call me when she gets back home." Jemma nodded as she placed her hands on his slim waist.

"Do you want to talk about it?"

"No, I'm good, babe. I promise." She nodded as Will started to play with her left hand.

"I should probably heat up the food."

"Leave it. I'm hungry for something else," he said against her neck.

"Will, what are—"

She looked down to see why he was still messing with her hand, and she saw him slip on a diamond-studded engagement ring. Her heart fluttered at the piece of jewelry, and she gasped. It fit her finger perfectly, and the diamonds were sparkling radiantly.

"Oh my God," she whispered, still not believing what she was seeing. Will stepped back to look at her and saw her eyes become glossy with unshed tears.

"Marry me, Jemma. Complete my life," he said in a low, sexy voice. She looked up at him. Her beam mirrored his.

"Yes. I'll marry you, Will. I love you so much."

"I love you, Jemma." They held each other again as their lips connected; Will beyond happy that she was going to be his wife.

A FEW DAYS LATER, Will had pulled up in front of Michael's parents' house in Oakbrook Terrace, and Jemma peered at the exterior of the huge mansion. It was a nice, sunny day, and they walked with their hands clasped together while striding toward the rear of the house. Mr. Vy had called and invited Will to a celebratory BBQ in honor of Michael being free. Will had told him that he didn't want to impose on the family outing, but he insisted that Will make an appearance.

Jemma was wearing a yellow and white polka dot summer dress, and Will had on light colored blue jeans and a white and gray plaid shirt. When they got to the backyard, there was music playing, and people were walking around, eating, and playing games. There were two blue plastic tents up to provide shade for those who didn't want to sit under the sun. Two big grills were lit and cooking a variety of meats, and three long tables of food and drinks were set up along the fence.

"This is a big gathering," Jemma said, noticing Michael was standing by the makeshift volleyball net, talking to some boys around his age.

"Yeah, it looks like they went all out," Will commented. Mrs. Vy spotted Will and walked over to him, giving him a long hug.

"Thank you for coming, Mr. Rutherford."

"Thank you for the invite. This is my fiancée, Jemma." They greeted each other, and she signaled for her husband and son. Mr. Vy welcomed Will and Michael exchanged some words with his former lawyer.

"Excuse me. Can I get everyone's attention?" The music was lowered, and all the partygoers looked toward their host.

"This is Mr. William Rutherford, and this young man is the reason why we're here today. He's the attorney who worked on Michael's case and proved his innocence. I will be the first to admit his age had me worried because I didn't think he was up to the part and he'd just half-ass it. He proved me wrong, and I want to offer my apology for doubting him. Please, join me in a round of applause."

Mr. Vy said proudly, and Jemma smiled as loud cheers were extended to Will as Mr. Vy took him around to meet the rest of the family. Long after the sun had set, the party was still going full swing. Some people had left, but the majority was still hanging around, enjoying the free food and beverages. Jemma was sitting at a table by herself, enjoying the scene. She had played several games of cards, ate some food, and conversed with different people at the party. Mrs. Vy sat across from Jemma, and she smiled at the married woman.

"Enjoying yourself?"

"Yes, ma'am. This is a nice party."

"We just wanted to celebrate after the past stressful weeks." Jemma nodded and cleared her throat before speaking.

"I hope I'm not overstepping, but have you spoken to Tilda since the trial?"

Mrs. Vy shook her head and sighed. "Sadly, no. We've tried to call and went by her apartment. She was never comfortable with being a boy, even when she was little. She started changing to fit her gender when they were younger. I guess we never thought about that male part of her," Mrs. Vy confessed. She was talking to Jemma but looking at everything that was going on around them.

"I work at a hospital, and they have a network of support groups and counselors through social services that can help with her transition and the tragedies she's experienced losing Diana and their child."

Jemma gave Mrs. Vy the hospital business card, and she looked at it.

"Do you really think they can help her?" Mrs. Vy asked in a whisper.

"Absolutely. The social workers are trained to help anyone in any capacity, and they won't turn her away. Will she be charged?"

"We've talked to the ADA. The death was ruled an accident, and there was no intent. She'll get probation and will have to do community service. The Lakes' appeal on her part helped the ADA come up with the decision."

"I hope everything works out for you and the Lakes," Jemma said honestly, and Mrs. Vy let out a small smile.

"We'll just take it one day at a time."

Marvin Gaye's "Got to Give It Up" came on, and all the older folks got excited and began to dance. Jemma grinned when she saw Mr. and Mrs. Vy dancing together. Will slid into the chair next to her.

"Hey, you."

"Hey, yourself. You're a celebrity here, Mr. Rutherford."

He smiled sheepishly at that. "Apparently, I've got the whole Vy family on retainer." She chuckled and took his hand.

"They really are thankful for what you did."

"I was just doing my job, sweetheart."

"So, what is Michael going to do now?" Jemma asked, glancing at the young guy.

"He's thinking about playing ball overseas." She nodded and watched the older couples boogying, and she grinned again. "You think that'll be us in a few years?" she asked Will, who turned to face her.

"Absolutely. I'm looking forward to it. Married life, kids, careers, grandbabies, retirement. Years of marvelous sex." Jemma rolled her eyes at that last part with a laugh.

"I promise to be a good wife to you," she said with a solemn tone, her eyes watching him.

"And I vow to be the best husband and provider to you," Will returned, his manly voice causing her to shiver.

"I might drive you crazy, Will. I'm just being honest."

"Oh, I know you will. I'm looking forward to all the craziness, and we're going to face it together."

"I like the sound of that," she said before leaning over to give him a slow peck.

EPILOGUE

YEARS LATER...

Jemma closed her eyes, enjoying the bubbling hot water from the jacuzzi. She had a rare moment of silence, and she wanted to take advantage of it. As soon as Will had left with the kids, she had rushed to run some bath water, relinquishing the candles and soft music she usually included. She adored being a wife and mother, but having five teenagers in the house... free time was most welcomed. Their brown cocker spaniel, Clover, pushed his way into the spacious bathroom and looked up at her.

"Hey, Clover. Mama can't get fifteen minutes, can she?" He cocked his head to look at her and wagged his tail, prompting Jemma to smile.

Clover was a gift from Will when he was only a puppy, and he was much-loved by the Rutherford clan. After spending a few more minutes enjoying the bath, she got out and dried herself off. Jemma went into the huge walk-in closet and sat on the silver, striped chaise to lotion her body and put on a white cotton shirt with matching capris.

"Okay, let's go feed you," Jemma said to the dog, who had sat down at her feet.

They had a massive two-story house in Orland Park with a

finished basement, a huge backyard, and a concrete driveway where the boys would sometimes play basketball with Will. The main bedroom was in the east wing of the house, and the kids' bedrooms were in the opposite wing with the girls sharing one room and the boys in the other one. Will and Jemma made sure the rooms would be spacious enough for them to have their own area and not be piled on each other. With all the kids, it was a total of five—three boys and two girls.

There was Will Joshua, the oldest, Steven Kenneth, who was named after Jemma's dad, Donovan Griffin, and the twins, Jessa and Tessa. When they found out their last pregnancy was a double, Jemma was so surprised that she had passed out. She didn't know it was possible, and Will thought it was funny. It wasn't until then that he told her that his great-grandmother on his mother's side had been a twin. After their wedding years ago, Will and Jemma waited three years before starting a family.

They happily admitted that they loved their time when it was just the two of them, knowing it would decrease after they had children. For her age, Jemma looked good without being vain about it, and she kept herself fit by using the gym equipment that was in the basement. She didn't have the body of a woman who had been through five pregnancies, and she was still madly in love with Will. Their marriage was a great one, and they were both happy.

Walking down to the ranch-style kitchen, she went into the pantry and grabbed the dry dog food.

"There you go. Such a good doggie."

She gave the dog a few pats on the head and went to the stand-alone island with a spatula in her hand. Jemma had made two dozen peanut butter cookies for her offspring and had let them cool off while she was upstairs. It was New Year's Eve, and they were spending it at home. The husband and wife had gone out for plenty of parties in the past and were content on bringing in the holiday at home with their rambunctious teens. She had turned on the satellite radio that was attached to the wall, and Donna Summer was playing on the disco station.

While she was transferring the cookies to a platter, she heard the garage door open, and she sighed with contentment, knowing the quietness was about to end, but she didn't mind. Clover sat at attention when the connecting door opened, and Will Jr. walked in first with some grocery bags.

"Hey, Ma."

"Hey, son."

"Dad got hit on by the woman at the video store," he said, taking a cookie. Will Jr. was the spitting image of his dad but had her eyes.

"What?" she asked, laughing.

He left the kitchen and went to take his coat off. Jemma knew she was about to hear the same story multiple times, and she shook her head. The youngest son, Donovan, walked in carrying three pizza boxes.

"Mama, some old lady told dad to call her when we were renting videos," Donovan said, placing the food on the glass table.

"Really?"

"Yep."

Their friend, Kevin, who was spending the night came in, carrying a bookbag with clothes in it.

"Hi, Mrs. Rutherford."

"Hello, Kevin."

"My parents said thanks for letting me spend the night."

"It's no problem."

He left, and Steven came in with video bags and more groceries.

"Hey, honey."

"Guess what? Some woman gave dad a 'come-get-me' look."

"You don't say?"

"But don't worry, Ma. She was old enough to be our grandmother."

He put the bags down and followed his brothers out the room. Tessa, Jessa, and their friend, Erica, came in; a mass of bubbly girl-ness.

"Hey, girls," Jemma greeted them, smiling at her daughters.

"Mama, oh my God! You missed it! This older lady was totally hitting on Dad."

"She had spiked hair and everything!"

Jemma looked between the twins as they spoke energetically.

They looked exactly like her but had their dad's green eyes. Will knew his girls were growing up, and they had to make their way in the world, but if anyone, a guy especially, made one of them cry, that would be their ass!

"Maybe I should go pay this woman a visit," Jemma replied, and Erica laughed.

"You're funny, Mrs. R. Thanks for letting me spend the night!" she yelled as the twins dragged her out the warm room. Erica was Jessa and Tessa's best friend, and she was spending a few nights over as well.

"Seven teenagers... definitely need some wine," Jemma said under her breath, placing dishes in the sink.

Will casually walked in with three more pizza boxes, and her heartbeat increased when she saw him. He had on a black skullcap with a sailor's coat on. He had a little gray sprinkled through his hair, which added to his sexiness.

"Hey, babe."

"Hi. I heard about your adventures at the video store."

He shook his head, taking off his outerwear and boots. "I figured the children might say something."

"Look at you, picking up teenagers and food while being mauled by an older woman."

"It's what I do," he stated, shrugging and she giggled while helping him unload the grocery bags.

"What did you get?" she asked, giving him a bump with her hip.

"Bought us some champagne for when the clock strikes midnight, some sparkling white grape juice for the teens, cheesecake for you, and snacks for them."

"Yeah, we should open the liquor right now," Jemma said, eying the bottle that he'd just put in the freezer.

Will was wearing jeans and a gray cashmere turtleneck. He had made partner a few years ago, and Jemma had become a charge nurse, making her one of the most revered members of the hospital. Jemma had gotten the family's last Christmas present that day, and she was anxious to show him.

Will reached out and grabbed Jemma by her hips and pulled his wife to him where they met each other's lips in the middle. Will was leaning against the chrome fridge, and his hands were sneaking down her back and traveled downward to gently squeeze her tushy. She wrapped one arm around his strong waist and placed her other hand over his heart. The boys, Kevin, Jessa, and Erica, came back into the room and saw their parents in a passionate cuddle.

"Aw man!"

"C'mon, Dad. We have company."

"Not in the kitchen."

Jemma turned around in front of her hubby while he licked his lips; Will placing his hands on her shoulders.

"Hey, Mrs. Rutherford, Steven said you'd make your famous pancakes tomorrow," Kevin said, and her eyebrows shot up while looking at Steven, who nodded.

"That's doable. Listen, I know it's New Year's Eve, and you seven can have all the fun you want, but I have two rules: don't tear up my house, and keep it clean."

The bunch agreed, and they grabbed the food boxes, video bags, soda, and paper plates and headed downstairs. The basement was carpeted with a massive sectional sofa, a working fireplace, pool table, full bathroom, projection size TV with a DVD player, VCR, and the latest game systems.

"I have something for you, Will."

"You do?" he asked with surprise.

"Yep, it's upstairs." She took his hand and went toward their bedroom.

"I know what the surprise is," he said as they stopped in their bedroom doorway.

"Oh, you do? What is it?"

"You're pregnant again." Will said, and she gasped, reaching out to slap his arm.

"What? No! That is not it!"

"Don't look like that. You don't want to have any more of my kids?" She threw her hands on her hips and cocked her head to the side.

"You know that's not the case. I love being the mother of your children, but I gave you five. Now, you're just being greedy."

Will rumbled with laughter and pulled her into the room where he closed the door with his foot. She went to the nightstand and held up a key and a piece of paper out to him. He read it after taking the items, and she grinned when she saw his facial expression.

"You got it?" Will asked, astonished looking at the deed to their vacation home that had been purchased in the Bahamas.

"Yes. I wanted to keep it quiet in case the deal didn't go through. I figure once the weather gets nice... maybe for summer break we can take the kids down there and have a month-long family vacation."

"Hell yeah!" Will dropped the deed that was in both of their names and wrapped a hand around her neck to bring her to him where he began to kiss her.

They had talked about purchasing a retreat home, but it was never finalized. He was happy about it and knew the kids would be overjoyed at the news. Jemma helped him take his sweater off and went to undo his belt. They walked back toward the bed, still kissing. He sat on the bed watching her tug her pants down before she got down on her knees. He ran his fingers over her hair, and she lowered her head to his dick after unbuttoning his jeans. She eagerly took him into her mouth, taking her time with the appendage. He leaned back on his hands and closed his eyes. His stomach muscles jumped when she deep throated him. Tessa knocked on the door, and she raised her head.

"Mom? Dad? We're starting the movie now," the twin said after she knocked.

"I didn't say stop," Will whispered to Jemma, and she dropped her head again.

"We'll be down in a few minutes, honey." Tessa went downstairs, and Jemma continued her oral loving.

After a few minutes, Will shifted her to that she was bouncing up and down on his shaft with her back to his chest. Both of them were amazed that they still had sexual magnetism after all these years. After they had amazing orgasms and fixed their clothes, they went down to the basement together. Will looked at his brood spread out all over the area, and he sighed as serenity passed over him.

He had a good life… a damn good life and wouldn't give it up nor take it for granted in any way. He had a wife he absolutely worshiped and was the very core of his heart, healthy kids who excelled in school, and a great career. Paris and Stan were still doing well and living in D.C. The kids were able to spend time with their wacky aunt who had flown into town for a few days for Christmas.

Jemma had one hand on her hip and was looking at each kid. She had love in her heart for all five of them equally. Will bent down and kissed Jemma on the forehead as they stood in the doorway.

"Thank you."

"For what?"

"For giving me all this, Jemma. For making my life… utterly wonderful."

She smiled at him, hugging his side.

"You're welcome, darling. Thank you as well."

As if drawn by a secret signal, all five of the Rutherford teenagers looked at their parents and smiled lovingly.

Catch Robert's Story in Rutherfords' Joy: A Family Legacy

LIKE OUR PAGE!

Be sure to LIKE our Major Key Publishing page on Facebook!

Made in the USA
Middletown, DE
03 May 2019